EXPLORERS : Gem Of Life

By Rashmitha Jayawardhana

CONTENTS

A concept art I got

SYPNOSIS

"In a world where magic and mystery coexist, 'Gem of Life' tells the tale of three extraordinary teenagers thrust into an extraordinary quest. Their kingdom is in turmoil as a malevolent queen, fuelled by dark ambition, steals the legendary Gem of Life-a mystical artifact with the power to turn all living beings into stone statues.

As their loved ones, friends, and even strangers succumb to the queen's curse, the trio embarks on a perilous journey through enchanted forests, fraught with treacherous trials and strange alliances. Their mission: to recover the stolen gem and break the queen's curse. Along the way, they encounter ancient trees that whisper riddles, confront their deepest fears, and unravel the secrets of a magical realm.

With time running out and the queen's power growing with each petrified victim, the young heroes must summon their inner strength to defy the encroaching darkness. 'Gem of Life' is an epic adventure of resilience, courage, and the enduring power of hope in the face of insurmountable odds. Can they restore life to their realm and discover the true meaning of friendship and bravery, or will the world remain forever frozen in stone?"

About the Novel - "Gem of Life":

In Rashmitha. J's latest masterpiece, "Gem of Life," readers are transported to a mesmerizing world where magic and mystery converge. The story follows three remarkable teenagers thrust into an extraordinary quest.

When a malevolent queen steals the fabled Gem of Life, an artifact capable of turning all living beings into stone statues, chaos engulfs the land. As loved ones are frozen in time, our heroes must navigate treacherous forests, face daunting trials, and form unlikely alliances on their mission to recover the stolen gem and shatter the queen's curse.

With the clock ticking and the queen's power growing, "Gem of Life" is a breathtaking adventure of resilience, bravery, and the enduring power of hope in the face of insurmountable odds. Rashmitha's storytelling prowess shines as he takes readers on a spellbinding journey through a world where friendship and courage hold the key to unlocking the frozen hearts of an entire realm.

About The Author

Rashmitha Jayawardhana

Rashmitha Jayawardhana is the creative mind behind Explorers - the Gem of Life, an Adventure novel that has captured the hearts of readers around the world. With a passion for storytelling and an insatiable imagination, Rashmitha Jayawardhana brings characters and worlds to life with their words.

Rashmitha Jayawardhana was born and raised in Sri Lanka. From an early age, he displayed a deep love for storytelling, often losing themselves in the pages of books and crafting their own imaginative tales. Their journey as a writer began as a childhood dream, and over the years, that dream evolved into a passion.

After signing up on Wattpad he embarked on publishing a narrative romance fiction he wrote "The Choice Of Love" later he started writing the book Explorers Gem Of life which talks about three kids who embark on a journey to save the word from an evil queen named Asena.

As an author, Rashmitha strives to create narratives that not only entertain but also resonate with readers on a profound level. Their writing is a reflection of their deep fascination with of Fiction, Adventure and Romance , and they are committed to exploring the human experience through the lens of books.

When not immersed in the world of words, Rashmitha can be found Programming or watching movies , which often serve as a wellspring of creativity and relaxation. Which in fact led to the writing of his novel. He is a firm believer in the power of storytelling to connect people across cultures and backgrounds.

Rashmitha Jayawardhana is excited to share their latest work, Explorers Gem Of Life, with readers and looks forward to captivating and inspiring the imaginations of many.

Meet me on Wattpad'

 @Rashthebro
https://www.wattpad.com/user/Rashthebro

The map

The map that will continue through the story

CHAPTER 1

THE BEGINNING OF THE DOOM

The sun had just begun its ascent, casting a gentle, golden hue over the town of Emberwick. It was a typical morning, one that marked the start of another day in the lives of three friends: Celine, Christine, and Alex.

Celine and Christine shared a room in the cozy house they called home. The room was adorned with shelves filled to the brim with books, their spines a rainbow of colours and stories waiting to be explored. Celine, the elder of the two sisters, lay in bed, her chestnut hair fanned out on the pillow, and her green eyes fluttered open as the first rays of sunlight kissed her cheeks.

She stretched, welcoming the day with a soft smile, and glanced over at her sister's bed. Christine, her fiery red hair splayed across the pillow, was already awake and absorbed in a thick tome.

"Celine, it's time to wake up," Christine said without looking up from her book.

Celine yawned and stretched again. "You're always up so early, Chris. What's got your attention this time?"

Christine finally tore her eyes away from the pages and beamed at her sister. "The history of magical artifacts in the Enchanted Forest. It's fascinating stuff, you know."

Celine chuckled. "You and your books, Chris. I'll never understand how you can be so awake and enthusiastic this early in the morning."

Meanwhile, just next door in the neighbouring house, Alex was already in the midst of his morning routine. His room was a contrast to the sisters' cozy bookfilled haven. It was tidy, with a computer desk in one corner where his laptop sat, wires trailing neatly along the floor.

As Alex pulled on his sneakers, he spotted a programming book on his desk and couldn't resist giving it a quick read. Code snippets danced in his mind, and he muttered to himself, "I wonder if I can optimize that loop."

Downstairs, the aroma of freshly brewed coffee wafted through the kitchen. Celine and Christine's mother, Mrs. Whitethorn, was already busy preparing breakfast. She called up the stairs, "Girls, breakfast is ready! Alex, you're welcome to join us too."

Celine and Christine quickly dressed and headed downstairs. They joined their mother at the table, where a spread of pancakes, syrup, and fresh fruit awaited. Celine, ever the bookworm, had brought her current novel with her.

As Alex entered their home, he greeted Mrs. Whitethorn with a warm smile. "Morning, Mrs. Whitethorn. Thanks for the invitation."

Mrs. Whitethorn smiled back. "You're always welcome here, Alex. Sit down and eat. It's a school day, after all."

They chatted amiably over breakfast, discussing their plans for the day and the upcoming school assignments. Celine eagerly shared her thoughts on the novel she was engrossed in, her eyes lighting up as she delved into the intricate plot and complex characters.

"Have you reached the part where the protagonist discovers the hidden artifact yet?" she asked Christine, her voice filled with excitement.

Christine nodded, her own enthusiasm shining through. "Yes, it's just around the corner. The suspense is killing me!"

Alex couldn't help but smile as he listened to their animated discussion. "You two are like characters from a novel yourselves," he remarked. "Christine, you with your love for books, and Celine, your endless thirst for knowledge."

Christine beamed, feeling a sense of pride in her sister's intellectual curiosity. "And Alex," she added, "with your coding wizardry and love for problem-solving, you're the one who keeps our adventures grounded in the real world."

Christine chuckled. "Our own unique trio."

With breakfast concluded, the three friends gathered their belongings and headed out the door, ready to face the day ahead. The sun had fully risen, and the town of

Everhart buzzed with life, unaware of the extraordinary adventure that might await them.

The trio arrived at Everhart High School, a place that had witnessed their shared laughter, struggles, and countless adventures. With their backpacks slung over their shoulders, they headed straight for the library after depositing their jackets in their lockers.

The library was a sanctuary for Christine. Rows of bookshelves stretched toward the ceiling, their spines lined up like old friends waiting to be embraced. She claimed her usual corner table by the window, where the morning sun spilled in, casting a warm glow over her chosen spot.

Christine settled into her chair, her book already open to where she had left off that morning. Her eyes danced across the pages, devouring the tale of a brave sorcerer who sought to unravel the mysteries of an enchanted forest.

Meanwhile, Celine was engrossed in her own world. Her laptop sat before her, notes scattered across the screen as she diligently researched wildfires for a school project. Her fingers danced across the keyboard as she gathered information, her determination evident in her furrowed brow.

Alex, ever the tech-savvy coder, took out his laptop and settled at a nearby table. Lines of code flashed across his screen as he worked on his latest project. Algorithms and data structures were his passion, and he couldn't resist the allure of solving complex problems.

As Christine flipped through the pages of her novel, her fingers brushed against something unusual-a worn, leather-bound book hidden behind a row of thick tomes. Curiosity piqued, she pulled it out. The book felt ancient, its pages yellowed and edges frayed. Its title, "The Chronicles of Destiny," was embossed in faded gold letters.

Intrigued, Christine opened the book, revealing a handwritten introduction: "Year 2023, the Year of Destiny. Three souls, bound by fate, shall rise to face the greatest challenge of their lives. A stolen Gem of Life, one of the precious Life Stones that sustains our world, threatens to plunge all living beings into eternal stone. It is your destiny, dear reader, to embark on a quest to retrieve the gem and save our world."

Christine's eyes widened as she continued reading. The book explained that the Gem of Life was one of the Life Stones that formed the foundation of their world. These stones, scattered throughout the realm, held the power to sustain life itself. If one was stolen or lost, the balance of the world would be disrupted, and living beings would be turned to stone.

Excitement and disbelief coursed through her as she absorbed the ancient prophecy. Her heart raced with the realization that the year 2023 was upon them. This was the year of destiny spoken of in the book.

Unable to contain her excitement, she jumped up from her seat and hurried over to Alex and Celine. She held the book aloft, her voice trembling with a mix of awe and urgency. "Guys, you won't believe what I found!"

Alex glanced up from his code, raising an eyebrow. "What's got you so excited, Chris?"

Celine paused in her research and looked at Christine, curiosity etched across her features. "Yeah, what's going on?"

With a breathless laugh, Christine began to explain the contents of the mysterious book, recounting the prophecy and the theft of the Gem of Life by a villainous queen. She emphasized the part about three individuals being destined to save the world in the year 2023.

"But Chris, it's just a book," Alex said sceptically, his fingers still typing away. "A fantastical story, maybe, but not reality."

Celine nodded in agreement. "Yeah, it's intriguing, but we can't base our actions on something from a book, especially something as fantastical as this." Christine frowned, torn between her excitement and her friends' scepticism. She knew the story sounded far-fetched, but something about it tugged at her heart. The weight of destiny hung in the air, and she couldn't ignore it.

Reluctantly, she closed the book and set it aside. "Fine, maybe you're right. But what if it's true? What if we're meant to be the ones to save the world?"

Ignoring the lingering doubts, they gathered their belongings and headed to their first class, the mysterious book and its prophecy left behind in the library, like a distant echo of an unspoken destiny.

The trio entered their classroom, eager to dive into another day of learning. However, as they stepped inside, an eerie silence greeted them. The classroom was empty, not a single student in sight. It was as if the entire class had vanished into thin air.

Alex exchanged a puzzled glance with Celine, and they both frowned. "This is strange," Alex muttered. "Did we miss an announcement or something?"

Celine scanned the room, her eyes narrowing as she noticed something peculiar. "Look at the desks," she said, pointing at the rows of empty seats. "There's something on each one of them."

Christine, her conviction from earlier still burning within her, approached one of the desks and gasped. On the desk lay a small, smooth stone where a notebook and pen should have been. She picked it up, her fingers trembling. "These...these are stones," she stammered, her voice quivering.

Alex and Celine joined her, examining the lifeless objects on the desks. It was truethey were stones, polished and cold to the touch.

Alex shook his head, disbelief etched across his face. "This can't be real. It's like some sort of elaborate prank."

Celine's brow furrowed as she considered the situation. "But who could have pulled off a prank like this? And where is everyone?"

Christine clutched the book she had found in the library, her heart pounding. She believed, deep down, that the book held the answers. "Guys, I think the book was right. Something terrible has happened, and we might be the only ones who can fix it."

Alex, still skeptical, glanced at his watch. "This is insane. Mr. Reynolds is never late, not even by a minute. We should wait a bit longer."

Ten minutes passed, and the teacher still hadn't arrived. The once-empty classroom had become a chamber of silence, filled only with stone remnants of their classmates. The walls seemed to close in around them, suffocating with uncertainty.

Christine's voice trembled as she spoke, "Alex, you said Mr. Reynolds would never be late, even if he was to die in a minute."

Alex's face turned pale as he realized the weight of his own words. "You don't think..."

Celine placed a comforting hand on his shoulder. "Let's not jump to conclusions. We need to figure out what's happening. And Christine might be right-the book could hold the key."

With their hearts heavy and their minds racing, they decided to put their faith in the book and the destiny it spoke of, setting out on a path that would challenge their beliefs and lead them deeper into the mysteries of the Enchanted Forest.

Fear and unease hung heavily in the air as the three friends cautiously stepped out into the corridor. The once-bustling school was now an eerie, empty labyrinth of echoing footsteps and distant whispers.

Alex ran his hand along the lockers, the metallic clinks reverberating through the hallway. "This is unreal. Where is everyone?"

Celine, her camera slung around her neck, began to snap photographs of the deserted school. Each click of the shutter seemed to emphasize the eerie silence that surrounded them. "It's like everyone just disappeared."

Christine clutched the mysterious book tightly in her hands. Her conviction had grown stronger with each passing minute, and she couldn't ignore the nagging feeling that they were the only hope in this unsettling emptiness. "We can't stay here. Let's explore and see if we can find any clues."

They ventured further into the school, their footsteps echoing through the deserted halls. Lockers stood open, books and belongings left behind as if people had vanished mid-activity. Desks in classrooms were empty, their chairs pushed back as if the students had simply stood up and walked away.

The trio arrived at the school's main entrance, where sunlight streamed through the glass doors. They pressed their faces against the glass, peering out onto the streets of Everhart. To their shock, the town was just as deserted as the school.

"This can't be happening," Alex muttered, his voice trembling. "The entire town is empty. It's like a ghost town."

Celine's camera captured the haunting scene before them-deserted streets, empty cars, and storefronts with their doors ajar. "I've never seen anything like this. It's as if time stopped."

Christine, her eyes still fixed on the book, remembered the prophecy it held. She whispered to herself, "The Gem of Life, the Life Stones that make up our world... Could this be the result of the gem's theft?"

A sense of conviction burned within her. She believed that they were the ones destined to retrieve the gem, to restore life to their world. But she also knew they needed answers.

"We need to head deeper into the Enchanted Forest," Christine declared. "The book mentioned a quest, and I think it's our only hope to reverse whatever has happened."

Alex and Celine exchanged glances. Despite their skepticism, the emptiness that surrounded them was undeniable proof that something extraordinary was unfolding. They nodded in agreement, ready to embark on a journey that would challenge their beliefs and confront the mysteries of their world.

As they stepped out into the deserted streets of Everhart, the realization that they were the only living souls left weighed heavily on them. The Enchanted Forest loomed on the horizon, its towering trees beckoning them into the unknown.

The once-familiar path leading to the forest was now overgrown with tangled vines and thorny bushes, as if nature itself had risen to claim its territory. The entrance to the forest seemed both inviting and foreboding, the ancient trees whispering secrets to those who dared to enter.

With the book as their guide and the weight of destiny on their shoulders, they took their first steps into the Enchanted Forest, ready to confront the challenges that lay ahead and to unlock the mysteries of the Gem of Life. In the heart of the forest, they hoped to find the answers that would not only save their town but also restore life to a world turned to stone.

The quest had begun, and the fate of their world rested in their hands.

As the sun dipped below the horizon, casting long shadows across the deserted town of Everhart, the trio decided to head home to gather supplies for their impending journey into the Enchanted Forest. Christine's belief in their destiny had ignited a spark of hope, and they were determined to do whatever it took to reverse the strange phenomenon that had turned their world to stone.

The walk home was sombre, the empty streets echoing their footfalls. They reached Celine and Christine's house, and as they opened the door, the weight of the situation hit them with a crushing force. In the dimly lit living room, their mother, Mrs. Whitethorn, stood frozen in the midst of her daily chores, a duster in one hand and a cleaning cloth in the other. Her face bore a look of determination, as if she had been caught mid-sentence while admonishing them for leaving their shoes in the hallway.

Celine and Christine gasped in horror, their eyes welling up with tears. They rushed to their mother's side, but she remained motionless, her vibrant spirit trapped within a lifeless statue.

Their sobs filled the silent house as they hugged their mother's stone form. "Mom," Christine whispered, her voice trembling, "we promise to bring you back. We promise to fix this."

Celine's tears fell freely, her voice choked with emotion. "We won't let this be the end, Mom. We love you."

Alex, though deeply affected, remained strong for his friends. He placed a hand on Celine's shoulder and spoke softly, "We'll make it right, I promise."

Determined to honour their mother's love and their newfound purpose, they left the house, leaving behind a heartfelt note, and ventured to gather supplies for their journey.

Their first stop was the corner store next door. The once-bustling shop now stood silent and unattended. With a mischievous twinkle in his eye, Alex said, "Well, it looks like we have free reign here. Let's gather what we need."

Christine couldn't help but smile through her tears. "This is certainly one way to prepare for a quest."

They moved through the store, selecting food, water, and other essentials from the shelves. The absence of shopkeepers and customers made their "shopping spree" oddly comical. Alex juggled a stack of canned goods, pretending to be a master juggler, while Christine tried on an oversized sun hat, causing Celine to burst into laughter for the first time in days.

After successfully pilfering the store (with a silent apology to the absent shopkeeper), they gathered in the aisles to pack their supplies into backpacks. Celine and Christine meticulously organized food, water, and first-aid supplies, while Alex, with his technical skills, rigged a small GPS device to help them navigate the forest.

As they packed, Christine couldn't help but glance at the mysterious book. She opened it to the page with the map and traced a finger along the lines. "This map will guide us to the Gem of Life," she said with determination. "And with the supplies we've gathered, we're ready for whatever challenges lie ahead."

Their backpacks filled and their hearts heavy with resolve, the trio left the empty shop, each taking a final look at the world they once knew before venturing into the unknown. With the map in hand and their mother's frozen form imprinted in their memories, they set out toward the heart of the Enchanted Forest, ready to confront the challenges that awaited them and to restore life to a world turned to stone.

The night air was crisp as they made their way to the outskirts of town. Stars twinkled overhead, casting a dim glow on their path. The Enchanted Forest loomed before them, its ancient trees seeming to whisper secrets and beckoning them closer.

The journey ahead was uncertain, and the weight of their mission was heavy, but they knew they had each other. With their mother's love as their guiding light and the mysterious book as their map, they walked deeper into the forest, ready to face whatever challenges the Enchanted Forest held and determined to retrieve the Gem of Life to save their world from the grip of stone.

As they ventured into the unknown, their laughter, tears, and shared determination bound them together, forging a bond stronger than ever before. The path ahead would not be easy, but they were ready to embrace their destiny and, against all odds, bring life back to a world that had turned to stone.

The first night of their quest had begun, and they would continue to walk the path of uncertainty with unwavering hope and resilience, determined to reach the Gem of Life and change the fate of their world.

The moon hung low in the night sky, casting an otherworldly glow upon the deserted streets of Everhart. Celine, Christine, and Alex had packed their backpacks with supplies and set out on their bicycles, determined to begin their journey into the Enchanted Forest. The town's eerie stillness was broken only by the soft hum of their tires on the pavement.

Christine, her bike's headlamp cutting through the darkness, took the lead. In her hand, she clutched the mysterious book open to a page that showed directions. "According to the book," she said, her voice resolute, "we need to follow this road until we reach the forest's edge."

Alex, riding beside her, couldn't help but grumble. "You know, forests and technology don't really get along. What if we get lost, and my GPS goes haywire?" Celine, trailing behind, chuckled softly. "Alex, in an enchanted forest, I don't think your gadgets will be of much help."

He shrugged, a trace of scepticism in his voice. "Well, I'll do my best to keep us on the right path."

They pedalled through the empty town, the night air crisp and cool against their skin. As they drew closer to the forest, the darkness deepened, and the ancient trees seemed to stretch taller, their branches weaving a shadowy tapestry above.

At the forest's edge, Christine came to a halt, her bike's headlamp casting an eerie glow on the dense foliage. She consulted the book's directions and spoke with determination, "This is it. We dismount here and proceed on foot."

Alex sighed, propping his bike against a tree. "I can't believe we're doing this," he muttered, clearly uncomfortable with leaving behind the comforts of technology.

Celine, the voice of reason, gave him a reassuring pat on the shoulder. "We're in this together, Alex. And who knows, maybe this forest will surprise you."

Christine led the way, holding the book aloft like a guiding lantern. The forest enveloped them in an unsettling silence, punctuated only by the occasional rustle of leaves or the distant hoot of an owl.

As they followed a narrow, winding path, the towering trees formed a natural canopy above, their branches interlocking like an intricate puzzle. Moonlight filtered through the leaves, creating a magical, almost dreamlike ambiance.

Alex couldn't resist a comment as they ventured deeper into the forest. "You know, this place could really use some Wi-Fi. And I've got no signal at all."

Christine chuckled softly, her voice carrying a sense of wonder. "That's the beauty of it, Alex. We're stepping into a world untouched by modern technology, where nature reigns supreme."

Celine, always the observer, marvelled at the forest's natural beauty. "Look at these trees, their roots firmly embedded in the earth. It's as if they've been guarding this place for centuries."

They continued their trek, with Christine consulting the book's directions and leading them deeper into the heart of the Enchanted Forest. The path twisted and turned, and the eerie silence began to feel strangely comforting.

Hours passed, and fatigue started to settle in. They decided to take a brief respite, finding a moss-covered rock beside a gentle stream. Celine unpacked the provisions they had taken from the shop-a mix of snacks and canned goods.

Alex inspected the assortment with a raised eyebrow. "Not exactly a gourmet meal, but it'll do."

Christine, still clutching the book, spoke softly as she gazed at its pages. "This map guides us, but it doesn't reveal the challenges that await. We must be ready for anything."

Celine nodded, her gaze fixed on the stream. "And we must never forget our purpose-saving our town, our world, and our mother."

They ate in silence, their thoughts consumed by their mission and the enigmas that lay ahead. The forest had grown darker, and the sounds of nocturnal creatures filled the air.

After their brief rest, they resumed their journey on foot. The path steepened, and the forest seemed to close in around them, its ancient trees creating an almost mystical atmosphere.

As they walked, Christine's voice filled with determination. "According to the book, we're nearing the heart of the Enchanted Forest where there is an oak tree. That's where we'll find the Gem of Life."

Alex, despite his earlier skepticism, couldn't help but be awed by the surroundings. "I have to admit, this place is like nothing I've ever seen. It's like stepping into a myth."

Celine smiled, her eyes reflecting a quiet determination. "We may not have all the answers, but as long as we have each other, we can face whatever comes our way."

The trio pressed forward, their spirits unwavering, ready to confront the mysteries and challenges that awaited them in the heart of the Enchanted Forest. The path grew darker, but their hearts burned with hope and the belief that they could retrieve the Gem of Life and save their world from the grip of stone.

The night was long, and the forest's secrets were yet to be unveiled, but they journeyed onward, their footsteps echoing through the ancient trees. With Christine leading the way and the mysterious book as their guide, they were prepared to embrace their destiny and embark on the quest to gain the gem from the villain

As they looked at the circular indentation in the forest floor, a soft, radiant glow began to emanate from the ground, casting a warm light on their faces. The journey had been long, but they had finally reached the heart of the Enchanted Forest, where their true adventure would begin.

The Gem of Life awaited them, and with hope in their hearts and a deep sense of purpose, they began to descend into the earth, ready to face whatever challenges and mysteries lay hidden in the oak tree

to be continued in the next chapter

CHAPTER 2

THE FIRST GAME

As Christine, Celine, and Alex ventured deeper into the Enchanted Forest, their journey took them along winding paths that seemed to lead them further into an ancient world untouched by modern civilization. The moonlight filtered through the dense canopy of leaves, casting mysterious shadows on the forest floor.

Christine continued to lead the way with the book as her guiding light, while Celine and Alex followed closely behind. They walked in silence, their footsteps echoing softly in the quiet of the night.

Alex, however, couldn't resist the urge to voice his complaints. "This place is seriously creepy," he muttered, his voice carrying a hint of frustration. "And it's not just the lack of Wi-Fi. I mean, who goes on a quest in the middle of the night through a forest?"

Celine couldn't help but smile at his grumbling. "Alex, you've got to admit, there's something enchanting about this place. It's like we've stepped into a world from a storybook."

He let out an exasperated sigh. "I get it, Celine. It's all mysterious and magical, but I'd feel a lot better if we had some kind of plan. What are we even looking for, aside from trees and more trees?"

Christine, leading the way, chimed in with a hint of excitement in her voice. "According to the book, we're looking for clues, signs, anything that will lead us to Asena and the Gem of Life. We have to trust in the guidance of the forest."

Alex shot her a sceptical look, but he didn't argue further. He knew that he was part of this quest now, and it was more than just a fantastical adventure; it was a mission to save their town and their loved ones.

As they continued to walk, the forest seemed to take on a life of its own. Strange, glowing insects danced in the air, and the soft murmur of the stream they followed added to the surreal atmosphere.

Celine, always the observer, couldn't help but marvel at the beauty of the natural world around her. "Look at these fireflies," she whispered in awe. "It's like they're guiding us through the darkness."

Christine nodded, her gaze fixed on the book in her hand. "The forest has its own way of guiding those who seek its secrets. We have to remain open to its mysteries."

Alex, though still wary, couldn't deny the enchantment of the scene before him. "Okay, I'll admit it's pretty cool, but I still wish we had a more concrete plan."

Their journey continued through the night, each step taking them deeper into the heart of the Enchanted Forest. The forest's mysteries remained hidden, but their determination to find Asena and the Gem of Life burned brighter than ever.

As they walked, Alex's complaints gradually gave way to a sense of wonder. The forest, with its ancient trees and mystical aura, began to work its magic on him. He started to see the beauty in the shadows, the secrets in the rustling leaves, and the promise of adventure in every step.

Celine, noticing the change in his demeanour, couldn't help but tease him gently. "Alex, I thought you were the one who loved solving puzzles and cracking codes. Isn't this like a giant, natural puzzle waiting to be solved?"

He grinned, his earlier frustrations fading away. "You might have a point there, Celine. Who needs Wi-Fi when you have the world's oldest forest to explore?"

Christine smiled, feeling a sense of unity among them. "That's the spirit. We're on this journey together, and we'll face whatever challenges come our way."

With their newfound sense of camaraderie and a willingness to embrace the mysteries of the forest, they continued their quest into the heart of the Enchanted Forest. The night was far from over, and the challenges they would encounter were still shrouded in uncertainty. But as they walked, the forest seemed to whisper secrets, promising that their adventure was only just beginning.

The trio, now standing at the threshold of the Enchanted Grove, found themselves entranced by the sheer beauty that lay before them. The grove was a mesmerizing tableau of nature's finest artistry.

Tall, slender trees with leaves that glistened like precious gems stretched their branches high into the night sky, forming a natural cathedral of greenery. Moonlight filtered through the leaves, casting a silvery glow that seemed to breathe life into the very air.

A lush carpet of wildflowers painted the forest floor in shades of lavender, indigo, and silver-blue. Their delicate petals swayed in the gentle breeze, releasing a subtle fragrance that filled the senses with an intoxicating sweetness.

Fireflies danced among the blooms, their bioluminescent glow creating a symphony of light that added to the grove's ethereal beauty. Their movements were like tiny stars that had fallen from the heavens, lending an otherworldly charm to the scene.

The trio stood at the edge of this enchanting wonderland, awestruck and humbled by the breathtaking display of nature's splendour. The forest around them seemed to come alive with a harmonious melody—a soft rustling of leaves, the distant chirping of crickets, and the gentle babbling of a nearby stream.

Alex, who had been the most sceptical member of their group, found himself utterly captivated. His earlier complaints had vanished into the night, replaced by a sense of wonder he couldn't ignore. "This...this place is incredible," he whispered, his eyes wide with amazement.

Celine, who had always been the bookish observer, was equally enchanted. "It's like stepping into a fairy tale," she said in hushed tones, her voice filled with a mixture of awe and reverence. "I never imagined such a place could exist outside of storybooks."

Christine, still clutching the mysterious book tightly in her hand, nodded in agreement. "According to the book, this grove is of great significance in our quest. We must explore it and seek the clues that will lead us to Asena and the Gem of Life."

As they ventured further into the grove, the forest seemed to embrace them with open arms. The air was filled with the delicate scent of wildflowers, and the soft grass beneath their feet felt like a welcoming embrace from the earth itself.

However, as they delved deeper into the grove, something unexpected occurred. Christine, who had been holding the book, opened it to find a blank page staring back at her. Her brow furrowed in confusion. "This is strange," she muttered. "The book was filled with text earlier, guiding us through the forest."

Celine, always curious, leaned closer to examine the empty page. It didn't take long for her to notice something extraordinary. "Look," she said, her voice tinged with excitement, "as we walk, the book writes."

Alex, equally intrigued, stepped forward, and to their amazement, words began to form on the previously blank page. The text appeared in elegant, flowing script, describing the grove around them, the path ahead, and the mysteries that lay hidden.

"It's as if the forest is speaking to us through the book," Alex remarked, his scepticism now replaced by a sense of wonder.

Christine nodded, her eyes scanning the book's pages as they continued to walk. "This is the forest's way of guiding us. We must follow the words it writes."

And so, they embarked on a journey where the book served as both their guide and their storyteller. As they walked, the book chronicled their progress, offering descriptions of the grove's sights, sounds, and even the emotions that washed over them.

The grove seemed to respond to their presence, with flowers blooming in their wake and fireflies swirling around them in a mesmerizing dance. The soft, lilting melody of the forest's song accompanied them on their path, as if the very heart of the grove beat in rhythm with their steps.

Celine couldn't help but smile as she read the book's descriptions. "It's like the forest is alive, and it wants to share its secrets with us."

Alex, who had once longed for the comforts of technology, now fully embraced the magic of the moment. "This is incredible. It's like we're part of a living, breathing story."

As they continued to walk, the book revealed more about their quest. It spoke of the challenges they would face, the tests of courage and determination that awaited them, and the importance of their bond as friends.

Christine, who had been their steadfast leader, felt a renewed sense of purpose. "We are on the right path. The forest is guiding us, and we must trust in its wisdom."

The grove stretched on endlessly, with each step unveiling new wonders. The book's pages filled with descriptions of the flora and fauna that surrounded them, the gentle whispers of the wind, and the ancient magic that permeated the air.

As they walked, they couldn't help but feel a profound connection to the Enchanted Forest. It was no longer just a place of mystery; it was a part of their journey, a living, breathing ally in their quest to find Asena and the Gem of Life.

And so, guided by the words of the book and the enchantment of the grove, they pressed on, ready to face whatever challenges lay ahead, knowing that they were not alone in their adventure. The Enchanted Grove was a testament to the wonders of the world, and they were determined to unlock its secrets and fulfil their destiny.

As Christine, Celine, and Alex continued to follow the guidance of the enchanted book, they soon found themselves standing before a mysterious gateway. It was an archway formed by overhanging branches, shrouded in the soft, silvery glow of the moonlight.

Christine opened the book, and to their amazement, the empty pages filled with a riddle:

*In the heart of this enchanted grove, A challenge awaits, a puzzle

to solve.

A labyrinth of illusions, both real and feigned,

To reach the centre, your wits must be trained.*

The trio exchanged glances, recognizing that this was the next step in their quest. The book had revealed a hidden path beyond the archway, leading them into the heart of the mysterious labyrinth.

As they ventured deeper into the labyrinth, they realized that it was a place of wonder and confusion. The trees themselves seemed to shift and rearrange, creating ever-changing pathways that led in all directions. Illusions played tricks on their senses, making it difficult to distinguish reality from fantasy.

The book continued to guide them, its pages updating with cryptic clues and riddles that hinted at the correct path. "We must stay focused and use our problem-solving skills," Christine advised, her voice steady despite the bewildering surroundings.

Celine, always the analytical thinker, studied the riddles and clues with a determined expression. "The labyrinth is designed to test our ability to distinguish truth from illusion. We must trust our instincts."

Alex, who had once been sceptical of their quest, now embraced the challenge with enthusiasm. "Let's do this, together. We've come this far, and we won't be defeated by illusions."

They followed the clues, solving riddles and overcoming traps that tested their quick thinking and teamwork. At times, the labyrinth seemed to shift and bend, but their determination kept them on the right path.

As they journeyed deeper into the labyrinth, the illusions grew more convincing. They encountered mirages of loved ones, heard voices whispering promises of comfort, and saw tantalizing glimpses of the artifact they sought. Each time, they had to rely on their bond and their growing understanding of the labyrinth's tricks to press forward.

As Christine, Celine, and Alex ventured deeper into the maze, the once-silent surroundings began to change. The dense hedges that formed the labyrinth's walls seemed to echo with voices—whispers and murmurs that filled the air with an unsettling presence.

Christine, holding the book tightly, exchanged a concerned glance with her friends. The cryptic message within the book had prepared them for trials and challenges, but it hadn't mentioned anything about the disorienting voices that now surrounded them.

Celine, the logical thinker of the group, furrowed her brow in concentration. "Do you hear that?" she asked, her voice barely rising above the soft murmurs that seemed to emanate from all directions.

Alex nodded, his face etched with a mixture of curiosity and unease. "It's like the voices of countless people, all talking at once. I can't make out what they're saying, but it's making it hard to think."

Christine, ever the determined leader, tried to remain focused. She knew that losing their concentration in the maze could lead to dire consequences. "We can't let these voices distract us. Remember our purpose and stay together."

But it was easier said than done. As they continued deeper into the labyrinth, the voices grew louder and more persistent. It was as if they were surrounded by an invisible crowd, each voice vying for their attention.

Celine, who had always been the voice of reason, found herself struggling to concentrate. "I can't think straight with all this noise. It's like they're trying to overwhelm us."

Alex, normally quick-witted and tech-savvy, felt a growing sense of frustration. "I'm used to solving problems, but this is like trying to code with a thousand distractions."

The labyrinth seemed to play tricks on them, its walls shifting and rearranging as if in response to the cacophony of voices. They found themselves at dead ends, retracing their steps, and struggling to decipher the clues provided by the book.

As minutes turned into hours, the relentless voices wore on their nerves. Doubts crept in, and they began to question whether they could overcome this particular challenge. But they knew that giving in to the voices meant failure, and failure was not an option.

Christine, with her unwavering determination, decided to take a different approach. She gathered her friends close and spoke loudly, her voice cutting through the din. "Listen, everyone! We're here for a reason. We have a purpose—to find Asena and the Gem of Life. These voices are trying to distract us, to make us lose our way. But we won't let that happen. We're stronger together."

Celine and Alex, reminded of their shared purpose and the bond they had forged, nodded in agreement. With renewed determination, they pushed forward, ignoring the voices that continued to swirl around them.

The labyrinth seemed to resist their efforts, throwing more challenges their way. But as they stayed focused on their goal and relied on each other, they began to notice a change. The voices, once overwhelming, began to fade into the background.

It was as if their unity and determination had disrupted the maze's attempts to confuse and distract them. They pressed on, navigating the labyrinth's twists and turns with a newfound sense of clarity.

After overcoming the disorienting voices within the maze, Christine, Celine, and Alex found themselves standing before a massive wall of intricate symbols and glyphs. It was a formidable barrier that stretched as far as the eye could see, with no visible openings or doors.

Christine opened the book, and its pages revealed a new challenge:

Before you lies a wall of code, To pass through it, the path must be showed. Three chances granted, so choose with care, Unlock the way, if you dare.
Celine examined the wall, her analytical mind racing. "It appears to be a complex encryption," she observed. "We have three chances to crack it and reveal the path forward."

Alex, who had been the coding enthusiast of the group, felt a surge of excitement.

"This is where my skills come into play. I'll decipher this code and get us through."

With a sense of purpose, Alex began typing on an ethereal keyboard that appeared before him—a digital interface formed by the magic of the Enchanted Forest. Lines of code flowed from his fingertips, creating intricate patterns of symbols and algorithms on the wall.

However, the wall seemed to respond to his efforts, shifting and rearranging in response to his code. It was as if the wall itself was a sentient entity, determined to challenge and confound him.

Celine watched with growing concern as Alex's first attempt failed. "It's adapting to your code, Alex. We need to be careful with our remaining chances."

Christine, always the voice of reason, urged caution. "Let's analyze the code carefully before making another attempt. We can't afford to waste our chances."

But Alex, determined to prove himself, dove back into the challenge without hesitation. Lines of code danced across the wall as he worked tirelessly to break through its defences.

Minutes turned into hours as the group watched in tense anticipation. Each line of code Alex entered seemed to be met with resistance, and the wall's complexity only grew.

Celine couldn't help but voice her concern. "We have only two chance left, Alex. We need to approach this with precision and strategy."

Sweat beaded on Alex's forehead as he continued to code, his fingers moving rapidly. He knew that their remaining chance was dwindling, but he couldn't bring himself to give up.

Christine, always the anchor of the group, placed a reassuring hand on Alex's shoulder. "Remember, we're in this together. We'll support you, no matter what." With renewed determination, Alex analysed the wall's shifting patterns and made his final attempt. The lines of code he entered were calculated and deliberate, forming a complex algorithm that seemed to defy the wall's defences.

For a moment, it appeared that he had succeeded. The wall shuddered and displayed a series of glowing symbols that seemed to point the way forward. Hope surged within the group.

But then, to their dismay, the wall's symbols shifted once more, rearranging themselves into an impenetrable barrier. .

Celine sighed, her disappointment evident. "We gave it our best shot, but the wall is unbeatable. Our chances are exhausted."

Alex, frustrated and defeated, stared at the wall in resignation. "I'm sorry, guys. I thought I could crack it, but it's like nothing I've ever encountered."

Christine, ever the optimist, placed a hand on his shoulder. "We may have failed this challenge, but our journey isn't over. We'll find another way forward."

As Christine, Celine, and Alex stood before the formidable wall of code, their last chance to decipher it seemed to slip through their fingers. The wall had defied all their efforts, and a sense of defeat hung heavy in the air.

But just as they were about to turn away, Alex's face lit up with a sudden realization. His eyes, once clouded with frustration, now sparkled with a newfound determination.

"I remember something," Alex exclaimed, his fingers itching to type. "An algorithm I came across a while ago. It's complex, but I think it might work."

Christine and Celine exchanged surprised glances. They had witnessed Alex's coding prowess before, but the wall had proven to be a formidable opponent.

Still, they trusted in his expertise and waited with bated breath as he began typing.

The lines of code flowed from Alex's fingers, each symbol and algorithm carefully selected and executed. It was as if he was in a trance, his mind fully immersed in the intricate dance of programming.

The wall, for the first time, seemed to respond differently. It displayed the symbols and patterns Alex had entered, but this time, they remained steady and unchanging.

Celine leaned closer, her analytical mind processing the unfolding code. "It's working," she whispered in awe. "Alex, you've done it."

Christine couldn't help but smile, her faith in their friend's abilities well placed. "You've cracked the code, Alex. You've found the way forward."

With a final keystroke, Alex completed the algorithm, and the wall's surface shifted once more. This time, however, it revealed a clear and unmistakable path forward, a corridor that led deeper into the maze.

The trio shared a triumphant cheer, their spirits lifted by their friend's ingenuity. They had faced a seemingly insurmountable challenge and emerged victorious, their bond as friends stronger than ever.

Alex, though tired from the effort, couldn't help but feel a sense of pride. "We did it, together. This journey is a testament to our friendship and our determination."

Christine nodded in agreement. "No challenge is too great when we stand united. Let's continue our quest."

With the wall of code behind them, they ventured further into the maze, their steps filled with renewed purpose and confidence. They knew that they were one step closer to finding Asena and the Gem of Life, and they were determined to face whatever challenges lay ahead with unwavering resolve.

Celine asked out of curiosity "What did you do this time?"

Algorithm X, as described by Alex, is a formidable and complex sequence of prime numbers and recursive functions. It's a digital key capable of unlocking even the most stubborn of digital locks. Designed to tackle puzzles with unpredictable patterns and adapt to shifting variables, Algorithm X represents the pinnacle of Alex's coding prowess. In their journey through the Enchanted Forest, it emerges as their secret weapon—a powerful tool that can decipher the maze's cryptic challenges and lead them one step closer to finding Asena and the Gem of Life.

It's a testament to the extraordinary abilities of their friend and a symbol of hope in the face of adversity.

As they disappeared into the labyrinth's depths, the echoes of their triumph reverberated through the maze, a testament to their unyielding friendship and their ability to overcome even the most complex of obstacles.

As Christine, Celine, and Alex continued their journey deeper into the heart of the Enchanted Forest, they gathered fallen wood to build a campfire. The dense canopy of ancient trees above cast eerie shadows, and the forest was eerily silent. Despite the gravity of their quest, they shared moments of respite and camaraderie.

Alex, stacking wood for the fire, quipped with a smile, "Who knew our adventure would turn us into expert wood gatherers?"

Celine, arranging the logs, joined in the humour, "Well, it's all part of the hero's journey, right? We'll add 'master campfire builders' to our list of skills."

Christine, kindling the fire, nodded with a touch of sadness in her eyes. "It's moments like these that remind us why we're here—to protect our world from darkness."

The fire crackled to life, and as the night settled in, they huddled around it, their faces illuminated by the dancing flames. They shared jokes and stories, laughter cutting through the heavy atmosphere of the forest.

Yet, beneath their cheerful banter, an unspoken sadness lingered—a recognition of the sacrifices and challenges they had already faced and those that still awaited them. But they were determined not to let their fears and doubts surface. They had come this far as a united front, and they would continue to do so.

With the fire crackling and the forest surrounding them, they set to work building their tents. Each pole and peg they hammered into the ground was a symbol of their resilience and resourcefulness. The tents, once raised, became their sanctuary in this mystical realm.

As night fell and the forest came alive with the sounds of unseen creatures, they retreated to their tents. Inside, the soft glow of lanterns cast a warm, comforting light. They settled into their sleeping bags, exhaustion washing over them.

Christine, her voice soft, said, "We've faced many challenges, and there are more to come. But as long as we're together, we can overcome anything."

Celine nodded, her eyes filled with determination. "We're stronger together, and we won't let anything stand in our way."

Alex, his gaze fixed on the tent ceiling, added, "Tomorrow is a new day, and we'll face it head-on. Rest well, my friends."

Though their hearts were heavy with the weight of their quest, they knew that rest was essential for the challenges that lay ahead. As they closed their eyes and drifted into slumber, they clung to the hope that each new day would bring them closer to finding Asena and the Gem of Life—their ultimate goal in this enchanted and perilous world

CHAPTER 3

RIVER OF MEMORIES

Morning sunlight filtered through the dense foliage, casting a warm, golden glow on the trio's campsite. They emerged from their tents, rejuvenated by a night's rest but burdened by the weight of their mission. As they sat around the remnants of their campfire, they engaged in a heartfelt discussion that would shape the course of their journey.

Christine, her expression serious, broke the silence. "We've made incredible progress, but we can't ignore the challenges that lie ahead. Asena is out there, and she possesses the Gem of Life. Our world, our loved ones, they're all depending on us."

Celine nodded in agreement, her eyes reflecting the gravity of the situation. "We need a plan. The Enchanted Forest is vast, and Asena could be anywhere. We must gather information, seek allies, and prepare for whatever confronts us."

Alex, his mind focused on strategy, chimed in, "We should also keep an eye out for clues, symbols, anything that might lead us to the Gem's location. The book mentioned that 2023 is our year to retrieve it, and time is running out."

With the decision to camp another day to regroup and strategize, they set to work. They examined the unusual book Christine had discovered in the maze, dissecting its contents and poring over the mysterious map within its pages. Celine's analytical skills shone as she deciphered the intricate symbols and hieroglyphs that adorned the map, searching for any hint of Asena's whereabouts.

While Celine and Christine delved into their research, Alex, ever the tech enthusiast, utilized the Enchanted Forest's magical properties to construct a magical communication device. This device, once completed, would allow them to communicate across the vast expanse of the forest, a vital tool in their quest.

As the day unfolded, they shared stories and theories about the Enchanted Forest's history. Legends told of its guardians, ancient beings with unique knowledge about the forest's secrets. They decided to seek out these guardians, hoping for guidance and insight that would aid them in their mission.

The decision to camp became a catalyst for unity. With their strengths and skills combined, they formulated a plan—a roadmap to find Asena and the Gem of Life. They would explore the forest, seeking clues, allies, and the guidance of the forest's guardians. The sun dipped below the horizon as they finalized their plans, their campfire casting long shadows, a reminder of the challenges that awaited them.

As the night settled in, they retired to their tents with a newfound sense of purpose. The Enchanted Forest, with all its mysteries and dangers, had become their realm of destiny. With resolve burning in their hearts, they drifted into sleep, ready to face the unknown of another day in this mystical land.

Under the vast canopy of the Enchanted Forest, Christine, Celine, and Alex settled into their respective tents. The sounds of the forest at night were a symphony of chirping insects, rustling leaves, and distant calls of creatures unknown. It was a stark contrast to the world they knew, a reminder of the otherworldly nature of their surroundings.

Inside their tents, they lay in their sleeping bags, their minds heavy with the weight of their mission. The events of the day, their discussions and planning, replayed in their thoughts. Each of them knew that their journey was fraught with uncertainty and peril, but they had found strength in their unity and determination.

Christine, in her tent, gazed at the faint glow of her lantern. She remembered the faces of her family, frozen in stone, and a deep sense of responsibility washed over her. The weight of the world rested on their shoulders, and the thought of failure was too much to bear. She clenched her fist, vowing to do whatever it took to save her loved ones.

Celine, ever the analytical thinker, reviewed the details of their plan in her mind. The mysterious book and its cryptic map were a puzzle waiting to be solved, and she couldn't rest until she had deciphered every clue it contained. She understood that their journey was just beginning, and the challenges ahead were unlike anything they had ever faced.

In his tent, Alex fiddled with a small, enchanted gadget he had created earlier in the day. It glowed softly, a testament to his ingenuity. He had always been the tech-savvy one, but in this mystical world, his skills were being tested like never before. As he closed his eyes, he hoped that the device would function as intended, connecting them with the forest's guardians and allies when the time came.

As the night deepened, they could feel the presence of the Enchanted Forest all around them. The rustling leaves and gentle sighs of the wind seemed to whisper secrets of the forest's past and its timeless mysteries. There was a sense that the forest itself was watching, waiting to reveal its secrets to those deemed worthy.

Despite the looming challenges, a sense of camaraderie and hope filled their hearts. The bonds of friendship had grown stronger, and their shared determination to bring their world back from the brink of darkness had become an unbreakable force.

As they drifted into sleep, their dreams were filled with visions of their loved ones, frozen in time. Each of them made silent promises to reunite their families, to save their world from the impending darkness. With that shared purpose, they found solace in the Enchanted Forest's embrace and a night's rest, knowing that a new day of adventure and discovery awaited them.

The Enchanted Forest began to stir with the first light of dawn. As the sun's rays filtered through the leaves, it cast a dappled pattern of golden light on the forest floor. Celine stirred in her tent, the gentle warmth of the morning coaxing her from sleep. She blinked away the remnants of dreams, her mind filled with determination.

Quietly, she unzipped her tent, slipped out, and stood amidst the ancient trees. The forest, as if acknowledging her presence, rustled in a gentle, welcoming breeze. Her eyes scanned the forest, eager to uncover its mysteries.

With each step, she felt the forest's magical aura wrap around her, whispering secrets in the language of the leaves. She was determined to explore, to seek answers, to take action. As she ventured deeper into the forest, her thoughts meandered into the peculiar and the amusing.

Unbeknownst to Celine, Christine's voice, tinged with sleep, echoed from her tent. "Celine, where are you going? It's barely dawn."

Celine, absorbed in her quest, called back, "I have to see what this forest holds.

There's a world of enchantment out here, Christine."

Alex's muffled response from his tent was equally drowsy. "Is it time for... coding?"

Celine chuckled at their half-awake inquiries, their words drifting into the forest. She marvelled at her friends' sleep-talking, a testament to the unusual circumstances they found themselves in. Her response was filled with humour, "No, Alex, not coding. Just a little forest exploration."

She continued her journey, and the forest seemed to come alive in response to her presence. The leaves danced in an intricate pattern, and a chorus of bird songs welcomed her. The Enchanted Forest was unlike anything she had ever seen, a realm where magic and reality merged seamlessly.

Celine's footsteps echoed through the woods, leaving a trail of wonder and curiosity behind her. She knew that the forest held answers, and she was determined to find them. The mysteries of this enchanting realm would not elude her, and she was ready to embrace every challenge it presented.

As Celine ventured deeper into the forest, her heart swelled with anticipation. She was surrounded by the unknown, and the enchantment of the Enchanted Forest beckoned her onward. And in the distance, the mischievous voices of her friends, still half-asleep, provided an unexpected touch of humour to their extraordinary journey.

As Celine's footsteps carried her deeper into the heart of the Enchanted Forest, she couldn't shake the feeling that this mystical realm held secrets beyond imagination. The leaves whispered ancient stories, and the trees seemed to lean in, sharing their wisdom in rustling voices.

As Celine's footsteps carried her deeper into the heart of the Enchanted Forest, she couldn't shake the feeling that this mystical realm held secrets beyond imagination. The leaves whispered ancient stories, and the trees seemed to lean in, sharing their wisdom in rustling voices.

The forest guided her, and as she followed a winding path, the air grew fresher and filled with the sweet scent of blooming flowers. A soft, melodious sound drifted to her ears, a gentle murmur that grew louder with each step. Curiosity kindled in her heart, and she quickened her pace, drawn toward the source of the enchanting melody.

As she rounded a bend, the forest opened up before her, revealing a scene of breathtaking beauty. There, beneath a shimmering canopy of leaves, lay the most extraordinary sight she had ever beheld—an enchanting river, its waters flowing with a liquid crystal clarity. The river was framed by luminous blossoms that lined its banks, their petals casting a gentle radiance, and the surface of the water rippled with an ethereal, silvery glow.

Celine's breath caught in her throat, and her eyes widened in awe. She had stumbled upon a place that could only be described as otherworldly—a river of pure magic, where time seemed to stand still.

As she approached the river, she dipped her fingers into the water, and it sparkled like liquid stardust. It was cool to the touch, invigorating as it caressed her skin. The foreshadowing was clear—this river held secrets, ancient and profound, and she was about to uncover them.

But there was more to this place than met the eye. The very air hummed with a mysterious energy, and the petals of the luminous flowers danced in a rhythm only they understood. She couldn't shake the feeling that there was a purpose to her presence here, a connection to the grand tapestry of the Enchanted Forest.

As she sat on the riverbank, the water's gentle melody filled her senses. Her mind raced with thoughts of what lay ahead in this mystical realm. The book she had discovered in the labyrinth, the map that held cryptic clues, and the river before her—all were pieces of a puzzle that begged to be solved.

Celine knew that the answers she sought were hidden within the heart of the Enchanted Forest, and this river was a gateway to its secrets. With

determination and a sense of reverence, she leaned in to listen to the soft murmurs of the water, hoping to decipher its ancient language.

Little did she know that her encounter with this enchanting river was merely the beginning of a journey filled with wonders and challenges beyond her wildest dreams. The foreshadowing she had sensed was a promise that her path was intricately tied to the mystical forces of the Enchanted Forest, and she was prepared to embrace the adventure that awaited her.

The river's crystal-clear waters glistened like liquid sapphire, reflecting the vibrant colours of the surrounding forest. It was as if each droplet held a fragment of the forest's magic, and the river's depths seemed to stretch into an abyss of unknown mysteries.

The petals of the luminous flowers that lined the riverbank swayed to an otherworldly rhythm, their delicate radiance harmonizing with the gentle murmur of the water. Their scent was intoxicating, a fragrant symphony that enveloped Celine in a sensory embrace.

She dipped her hand into the river once more, and as she lifted it, droplets cascaded from her fingers, shimmering like liquid starlight. The river's surface seemed to ripple with hidden knowledge, as if it held the stories of the Enchanted Forest, waiting for someone with the heart to listen.

In the distance, a soft breeze whispered through the trees, carrying with it a haunting, melodic tune. It was the forest itself serenading her, a melody that resonated with the deepest recesses of her being. This, she knew, was more than just a chance encounter—it was a foreshadowing, a glimpse of the profound and ancient secrets that lay hidden within the Enchanted Forest, waiting for her to uncover.

Celine's heart swelled with anticipation and reverence for the beauty and mystique of this place. She understood that her connection to the Enchanted Forest was no mere coincidence. It was a calling, an invitation to explore its wonders and uncover the truths that had remained veiled for countless generations.

As she sat by the river, her mind filled with thoughts of what lay ahead, of the quest to find Asena and the Gem of Life. She knew that the answers she sought were intricately tied to the enchantment of the forest, and this river was just the beginning of her journey. With determination and a sense of reverence, she leaned in to listen to the soft murmurs of the water, hoping to decipher its ancient language and uncover the profound secrets it held.

As Celine immersed herself in the wonders of the Enchanted River, her senses heightened by the river's ethereal beauty, she suddenly heard a deep and ominous growl that sent shivers down her spine. The harmonious symphony of the forest was shattered by the primal sound, and she knew that danger lurked nearby.

With a jolt, she sprang to her feet and scanned her surroundings. The onceidyllic riverbank had transformed into a place of imminent peril. Her keen eyes caught sight of a pair of fierce, amber eyes peering at her from the underbrush— a majestic and imposing tiger, its fur striped with patterns as enchanting as the Enchanted Forest itself.

Celine's heart raced as the tiger's growl intensified, a clear warning that she was intruding upon its territory. The river and its mysteries were forgotten as survival instinct took over. Without a moment's hesitation, she turned and sprinted back in the direction from which she had come, away from the tiger's looming presence.

The Enchanted Forest's dense foliage seemed to conspire against her, every branch and thorn threatening to impede her escape. Her breaths came in ragged gasps as she darted through the undergrowth, guided solely by her desire to reach her friends and alert them to the approaching peril.

Finally, she stumbled upon a familiar clearing, the site where their tents were pitched. She knew that Alex and Christine were still sound asleep, blissfully unaware of the danger that lurked in the forest. Celine's heart pounded in her chest as she understood the urgency of the situation.

With a sense of urgency, she knelt beside Christine's tent and shook her awake. "Christine, wake up! There's a tiger in the forest, and we need to leave now!" Christine, her eyes clouded with sleep, blinked at Celine for a moment before comprehension dawned. "A tiger? Are you serious?"

Alex, emerging from his own tent, rubbed his eyes and squinted at the commotion. "Is it time for... coding?"

Celine's voice trembled with fear as she urgently responded, "No time for jokes, Alex. There's a tiger nearby, and it's not friendly. We have to go, now!"

The urgency in Celine's voice spurred her friends into action. Christine swiftly roused herself, and the trio scrambled to gather their belongings. Tents were hastily dismantled, sleeping bags rolled up, and supplies gathered. The enchanting river, with its mysteries and ethereal beauty, was left behind, forgotten in the face of immediate danger.

As they packed in a frenzied hurry, the growls of the tiger drew nearer, a relentless reminder of the peril that pursued them. The majestic beast had detected their presence and was now hot on their trail.

Celine led the way, her heart pounding with every step. Her friends followed closely behind, their faces pale with fear but determined to outrun the imminent threat. The tiger's growls echoed through the forest, sending shivers down their spines.

The Enchanted Forest, once a realm of enchantment and wonder, had transformed into a place of danger and urgency. The lush undergrowth that had seemed so inviting only moments before now concealed lurking perils, and the once-gentle breezes carried a sense of foreboding.

Celine's mind raced as she navigated through the forest, searching for a path to safety. They needed to put distance between themselves and the relentless predator. Her thoughts were a blur of fear, determination, and the hope that they would emerge from this ordeal unscathed.

The tiger's growls grew louder, and the snapping of branches signalled its relentless pursuit. Celine's heart pounded as she led her friends through the forest, each step taking them further from the perilous presence behind them. The Enchanted Forest, with its enchantments and dangers, had become an unpredictable realm where every moment held the potential for adventure or peril.

Celine led her friends, Christine and Alex, deeper into the Enchanted Forest, their hurried footsteps echoing the urgency of their escape from the relentless tiger. The majestic beast's growls seemed to reverberate through the very trees, a constant reminder of the peril that pursued them.

As they raced through the forest, their breaths laboured and their hearts pounding, they encountered an unexpected obstacle. The forest path abruptly ended, leaving them trapped between a river, its crystal-clear waters shimmering in the sunlight, and the relentless predator closing in behind them.

Panic set in as they realized the severity of their situation. They were trapped on a narrow strip of land, and the river offered no refuge from the approaching danger. The tiger's presence was almost upon them, its growls a chilling reminder that they had run out of options.

Christine, her eyes wide with fear, looked around in desperation. "There's no way out! What do we do?"

Alex's voice trembled as he assessed their predicament. "We can't cross the river. It's too wide, and we don't know what dangers lie on the other side."

Celine's mind raced as she surveyed their surroundings. The river's enchanting beauty held no answers, and the forest offered no escape. It was then that her gaze fell upon the book they had discovered in the labyrinth, the very book that had foreshadowed their journey.

to be continued in the next chapter !

CHAPTER 4

The Second Game

With the Heartstone in their possession, Celine, Christine, and Alex continued their journey through the Enchanted Forest. The forest's magic seemed to resonate with the Heartstone's power, guiding them along a path that had once been concealed from mortal eyes.

As they journeyed deeper into the heart of the forest, they came across a large, tranquil river that blocked their path. The river's waters were clear and inviting, but their passage to the other side was impeded by the presence of water spirits—sentient beings of liquid grace that frolicked near the riverbank.

The water spirits, with their iridescent forms and voices like cascading waterfalls, were the guardians of this river. Their playful laughter filled the air as they danced above the water's surface. It was clear that crossing the river would not be as simple as it appeared.

Celine, Christine, and Alex observed the water spirits with a mixture of fascination and uncertainty. Thistle, the wise squirrel, sensed their hesitation and spoke, "To cross this river, you must earn the trust of the water spirits and demonstrate your respect for the realm they protect."

The Heartstone in Celine's hand began to glow softly, a sign that it held the key to this challenge. She opened the book they had discovered in the Enchanted Grove, and as its pages fluttered to a particular passage, they found themselves facing a riddle written in intricate script:

"In the realm where water spirits play,

To cross the river, you must find your way.

But to win their trust, you must first seek,

A treasure hidden where the waters speak.

To pass this trial and find your grace,

Bring the Heartstone to the river's embrace.

Whisper words of reverence and care,

The water spirits' secrets, they'll share."

The riddle posed both a challenge and a promise. To cross the river and continue their quest, they needed to discover the hidden treasure and gain the trust of the water spirits. Celine, Christine, and Alex exchanged determined glances, ready to embark on this new challenge.

With the riddle as their guide, they began to explore the riverbank. The grotto they entered was filled with an otherworldly aura, and they could feel the magic in the air as if it responded to their presence.

In the heart of the grotto lay a crystal-clear pool fed by a natural spring. The waters seemed to come alive, forming intricate patterns and symbols, a language of the river's secrets.

It was here that they found the hidden treasure—a delicate, luminous seashell resting on a bed of glistening pebbles. The seashell seemed to shimmer with an inner light, its iridescent glow revealing the depths of the water spirits' magic.

Christine carefully picked up the seashell, her fingers trembling with a sense of reverence. She whispered softly to the seashell, "Thank you for guiding us, for sharing your wisdom with us."

The water spirits, who had been observing their every move, seemed to acknowledge her words. With a shimmering dance, they beckoned the trio to the water's edge.

Alex, inspired by Christine's act of respect, joined in. "We honor your realm, your wisdom, and your guardianship of this river."

Celine, holding the seashell, spoke with heartfelt sincerity. "We promise to protect the Enchanted Forest and all its mysteries. Your secrets will remain safe with us." The water spirits, their forms radiant, surrounded the trio. They created a bridge of liquid light that spanned the river, leading to the other side. Celine, Christine, and Alex stepped onto the bridge, their feet supported by the magical waters.

As they crossed the river, they felt a profound connection with the water spirits and the river itself. The river, once a barrier, had become a passage filled with the spirits' approval and blessings.

On the far bank, the water spirits continued their enchanting dance, their laughter echoing through the forest. The trio had successfully earned their trust and moved one step closer to unravelling the forest's mysteries and finding Asena, the guardian of the stolen Gem of Life.

The path ahead remained shrouded in dappled forest light, hinting at more challenges to come. A cool breeze whispered through the leaves, and the trio knew that their adventure was far from over.

With the Heartstone in their possession, Celine, Christine, and Alex continued their journey through the Enchanted Forest. The forest's magic seemed to resonate with the Heartstone's power, guiding them along a path that had once been concealed from mortal eyes.

As they journeyed deeper into the heart of the forest, they found themselves on a narrow path that wound its way through the ancient trees. The air was thick with the scent of moss and wildflowers, and the leaves above created a dappled pattern of sunlight that danced across their path.

"Is it just me, or do these trees seem to be whispering secrets?" Celine mused, her gaze fixed on the towering trunks that surrounded them.

Christine nodded. "It's as if the forest itself is trying to guide us. I've read about ancient trees having a consciousness of their own."

Alex, ever the pragmatist, couldn't help but interject. "I think you've been reading too many fantasy novels, Christine. Trees don't have consciousness."

As they continued walking, the path became steeper, and the terrain more uneven. Their journey was accompanied by the rhythmic crunch of fallen leaves underfoot. The trio's steps were in sync, but their conversation soon turned playful.

Celine, always one for random facts, decided to share one. "Did you know that the world's oldest tree is over 4,800 years old? Imagine the stories it could tell."

Alex, trying to keep things light-hearted, chimed in, "I bet it would say, 'Stop talking and keep walking. We have a world to save.'"

Christine couldn't help but laugh at Alex's comment. "He's right. We've got a gem to find and a queen to stop. The forest can keep its secrets for now."

The trio continued their journey through the enchanting forest, weaving their way through ancient trees and allowing the playful banter to ease the weight of their quest. Though they faced challenges and uncertainties, they found comfort in each other's company and the simple joys of shared laughter.

As they journeyed deeper into the heart of the Enchanted Forest, the path became increasingly challenging. The terrain was uneven, and the uphill climb was taking its toll. The trio had been walking for what felt like hours, and fatigue was beginning to set in.

Celine was the first to voice her exhaustion. "I don't know about you two, but I could use a break. This forest feels like it goes on forever."

Christine nodded in agreement. "I second that. It's been a long journey, and I

can practically feel blisters forming on my feet."

Alex, always practical, suggested, "How about we take a short rest and then continue? We can't afford to linger for too long."

Celine, looking around, noticed a small clearing off the path. "Over there, that looks like a good spot to rest."

They settled into the clearing, and for a moment, the forest's enchantment seemed to lift. They felt the weight of their quest and the uncertainty of their path. The light-heartedness they had experienced earlier had given way to a sense of exhaustion and apprehension.

Suddenly, Christine, with a mischievous glint in her eye, spoke up. "You know, maybe we could use a break from all the seriousness. How about we play a game to pass the time?"

Alex raised an eyebrow. "A game? Here, in the middle of the Enchanted Forest?"

Christine grinned. "Why not? We need to recharge our spirits as much as our bodies. How about a game of hide and seek?"

Celine, despite her weariness, couldn't help but be intrigued by the idea. "Hide and seek in a mystical forest? That sounds both challenging and fun."

And so, they agreed to play hide and seek. They decided that Alex would be the seeker, and Celine and Christine would be the hiders. They each took a moment to find suitable hiding spots among the towering trees and underbrush.

Alex closed his eyes, counted to fifty, and then began the search. The forest seemed to come alive as they played, with the wind rustling the leaves and the occasional bird adding to the magical ambiance.

Celine, hiding behind a massive oak tree, found herself giggling softly. She couldn't remember the last time she had played hide and seek, let alone in such a enchanting place. As Alex's footsteps drew nearer, she tried to stifle her laughter, not wanting to give away her hiding spot.

Meanwhile, Christine had found a cozy nook nestled between the roots of an ancient tree. She watched with amusement as Alex passed by, clearly missing her concealed location. She held her breath and stifled a laugh, determined to remain hidden.

Alex continued his search, moving carefully through the forest. The Enchanted Forest seemed to play tricks on his senses, with shadows and dappled light making it even more challenging to spot his friends. He reached out to touch the bark of a particularly impressive tree, feeling the rough texture under his fingers.

Just as he was about to give up, a playful voice called out from behind a curtain of vines. "You found me, Alex!"

Alex turned to see Celine stepping out from her hiding spot. "Well done, Celine. You're a sneaky one," he said, offering a good-natured grin.

Celine laughed. "I had a great hiding spot, thanks to these old trees."

As they shared a moment of camaraderie, they heard Christine's voice from the distance. "Are you two ready to give up yet? Because I'm still hidden, and I have no plans to reveal myself!"

Christine's teasing tone spurred them on. They decided to continue their search, determined to find their friend. The forest seemed to work in mysterious ways, leading them in different directions and testing their friendship.

As they searched for Christine, they couldn't help but appreciate the unique beauty of the Enchanted Forest. The ancient trees, the vibrant flora, and the everchanging play of light made the journey feel like an adventure in itself.

Finally, after much searching and laughter, they discovered Christine's hiding place. She had perched herself on a moss-covered rock, her face a mix of triumphant and playful.

With a chuckle, Alex admitted, "You got us good, Christine."

Christine hopped off her hiding spot and joined the others, the playful atmosphere filling the forest with their laughter.

The trio sat down together, enjoying the sense of unity and joy that hide and seek had brought them. In the midst of their quest, they had found a moment of connection, playfulness, and shared laughter. It was a reminder that, even in the face of great challenges, friendship could light the way.

With their game of hide and seek behind them, Celine, Christine, and Alex shared a warm, heartfelt moment. They formed a tight circle, their arms wrapping around each other in a group hug. The embrace was filled with a sense of unity, a reminder that no matter the challenges they faced, they were in this together. "We make a great team," Christine said with a smile, her eyes reflecting a deep sense of trust in her friends.

Celine nodded in agreement. "We've come so far, and we'll keep going. No matter what the Enchanted Forest throws at us."

Alex, usually the reserved one, spoke up. "You're right. We've got this."

The forest around them seemed to respond to their unity, casting a warm, dappled light that seemed to offer its own form of encouragement.

With renewed spirits, they resumed their journey through the Enchanted Forest. Each step forward brought them closer to their goal, the stolen Gem of Life, and the chance to save their world from the grasp of the queen.

The forest's enchantment continued to guide them, and they ventured deeper into its heart, ready to face whatever challenges lay ahead.

As their journey through the Enchanted Forest continued, the trio began to feel the pangs of hunger. Their footsteps had taken them deeper into the heart of the forest, and they decided it was time for a well-deserved break to refuel their bodies.

They spread out in search of edible plants and berries, with the forest offering a rich bounty of nourishment. Celine, Christine, and Alex gathered a colourful assortment of forest treats, their eyes lighting up with the prospect of a satisfying meal.

Amid their foraging, the forest revealed an unexpected surprise. Nestled beneath a canopy of emerald leaves, they found a woven basket brimming with an array of delectable foods. The sight was as enchanting as the forest itself, and they exchanged bewildered glances. It was as though the very spirit of the forest had provided them with a feast, inviting them to partake in its mysterious generosity.

Curiosity got the best of them, and their rumbling stomachs urged them to explore the contents of the basket. The spread was nothing short of extraordinary: ripe, succulent fruits, freshly baked bread, aromatic cheeses, and sweet

confections that sparkled like stars in the night sky. It was a meal fit for royalty, and the forest seemed to have chosen them as its honoured guests.

The trio shared the meal, their taste buds dancing with delight at every bite. Laughter and stories flowed freely in the midst of their adventure. It was a reprieve, a moment of bonding and shared happiness that transcended the eerie magic of the Enchanted Forest.

As the day turned to night, they decided to make camp. They arranged their sleeping bags in a circle, encircled by the ancient trees. The forest's enchanting ambiance surrounded them, the gentle sway of branches and the soft rustling of leaves lulling them into a deep slumber.

However, their peaceful rest was soon interrupted by haunting dreams that visited each of them. In this shared nightmare, they found themselves suspended from the towering boughs of ancient trees, their hands bound by spectral vines that glowed with an eerie light. The air was thick with an unsettling tension, and the dim moonlight painted a chilling scene around them.

In the dream, they could feel the weight of their predicament, and a cold shiver ran down their spines. Their surroundings were an amalgamation of the Enchanted Forest's beauty and a lurking darkness. The atmosphere was heavy with a sense of foreboding.

As they dangled from the tree branches, the forest itself seemed to bear witness to their torment. The trees whispered secrets known only to them, their leaves rustling with eerie laughter. The haunting melody of the night creatures intensified their sense of unease.

In the dream, their voices were stolen by a mysterious force, and they couldn't communicate with each other. Panic gripped their hearts as they struggled against their ethereal bonds. The moon hung low in the sky, casting a spectral glow on their figures, and they felt a deep sense of dread as if their fates were intertwined with the forest's ominous magic.

The nightmare was relentless, an ordeal that seemed to stretch on for an eternity. It was a chilling reminder that the Enchanted Forest, with all its wonder, held secrets both beautiful and perilous. And in their dreams, they were confronted by the forest's darker side, a side that would test their resilience and courage.

As dawn's gentle light pierced the canopy of the Enchanted Forest, Celine, Christine, and Alex awoke from the haunting nightmare that had gripped their slumber. Each of them found themselves lying in their sleeping bags, drenched in cold sweat, and the memories of the dream still fresh in their minds.

They sat up in silence, the shared experience weighing heavily upon them. The unsettling dreams had left a residue of fear and confusion. The forest had gifted them a feast, but it seemed to hold a darker aspect as well.

Alex was the first to break the silence. "Did you all have that dream, too?"

Celine and Christine exchanged knowing glances, and Celine nodded. "Yes, it was as if the forest was showing us its mysterious and eerie side."

Christine added, "I felt a sense of foreboding in that dream. It's like the forest wanted to remind us of its power and secrets."

The trio's conversation circled around the implications of the dream. It was clear that the Enchanted Forest was a place of wonder and danger, beauty and darkness. Their quest to retrieve the stolen Gem of Life was not just a physical journey but a test of their resilience and determination.

After a moment of reflection, Celine spoke with determination in her voice. "We can't let the forest's mysteries deter us. Our world is depending on us to retrieve the gem and stop the queen. We have to move forward."

Alex and Christine nodded in agreement. The dream had been unsettling, but it hadn't shaken their resolve. They had come this far, and they were determined to see their mission through.

With renewed determination, they gathered their belongings, stowed away the remains of their mystical feast, and continued their journey through the Enchanted Forest. The forest's magic seemed to pulse around them, a reminder of the enchanting and unpredictable nature of their surroundings.

The beauty of the forest still captured their hearts, and the challenges it presented only served to strengthen their bond. They knew that, with each step they took, they were drawing closer to the stolen gem and the climax of their quest.

As they resumed their journey, they felt a sense of unity and purpose. The Enchanted Forest held both secrets and beauty, darkness and light, and they were determined to navigate its wonders and perils to save their world.

The forest whispered its secrets in the rustling leaves, and the trio listened, ready to face whatever challenges lay ahead on their path to destiny.

Their journey through the Enchanted Forest led them to a breathtaking sight—a colossal mountain that rose high into the sky, its peak concealed by a veil of mist. The mountain's majesty was awe-inspiring, and it cast a shadow over the forest, as if it held the secrets of the world.

Celine, Christine, and Alex gazed up at the towering mountain in both wonder and trepidation. It was unlike any mountain they had ever seen, and it seemed to pulse with an otherworldly energy.

Christine consulted the ancient book they had found in the Enchanted Grove. As she read, her eyes widened with understanding. "The book says we must climb this mountain to reach the gem. It's the next step of our quest."

The trio exchanged determined glances. They had come this far, facing numerous challenges and dreams that tested their mettle. The sight of the Enchanted Mountain served as a reminder that their journey was far from over.

With their trusty backpacks in tow, they began the ascent of the colossal mountain. The path ahead was steep and challenging, with rugged terrain that demanded their physical and mental strength.

The Enchanted Forest had brought them to this point, and the mountain represented another test of their determination and courage. The journey had revealed the depths of their friendship and their unwavering commitment to save their world.

As they made their way up the mountain, they knew that each step brought them closer to the stolen Gem of Life, and closer to their destiny.

TO BE CONTINUED!

CHAPTER 5

The Mystery Of A Hill

Their ascent of the Enchanted Mountain was arduous and unforgiving. Hour after hour, they climbed, their boots sinking into the rocky path as they pushed forward. The air grew thinner, and the sun beat down on them with unrelenting intensity.

Celine, Christine, and Alex were fuelled by determination and the knowledge that their mission was critical. The gem, and the fate of their world, awaited at the summit.

As they continued their gruelling climb, Celine began to show signs of fatigue. Her steps became unsteady, and her breath came in short, laboured gasps. Her friends noticed her struggle, and concern etched their faces.

Christine reached out to her sister. "Celine, are you okay? You don't look well."

Celine tried to muster a smile but failed. "I'm just tired, that's all. I can keep going."

Alex chimed in, his voice filled with worry. "Celine, there's no shame in taking a break. We're in this together, and we'll support each other."

Celine nodded and agreed to rest for a moment. She sat down on a boulder, her face pale, as she caught her breath. Christine and Alex shared a look, their concern deepening.

The Enchanted Mountain was relentless, and the trio had to dig deep within themselves to find the strength to continue. They knew they were on a mission that held the fate of their world in the balance, and they couldn't afford to falter.

After a brief respite, they resumed their climb. Celine pushed herself to keep moving, despite her exhaustion. The path seemed to stretch on endlessly, and the summit remained shrouded in mist.

As the hours passed, the exhaustion became unbearable. Celine's steps grew even more unsteady, and she swayed on her feet. She felt a wave of dizziness wash over her, and the world seemed to spin.

Christine and Alex rushed to her side as she collapsed to the ground, unconscious. Panic and fear gripped them, and they frantically tried to rouse her. Her pulse was weak, but she was still breathing.

"We need to get her down from here," Christine said, her voice trembling.

Alex nodded in agreement. "We can't continue the climb like this. We have to find a safe spot to rest and tend to Celine."

With great effort, they managed to carry Celine to a slightly more level section of the path. They made her as comfortable as possible, using their backpacks as makeshift pillows. The forest's magic, once wondrous and enchanting, now felt like an ominous presence.

The trio sat in silence, tending to Celine and watching over her. They knew that the Enchanted Mountain had thrown yet another challenge their way, and they were determined to overcome it.

With Celine now resting, her unconscious form lying on a bed of moss and leaves, Christine, and Alex were filled with a mix of worry and determination. They knew that their supplies were dwindling, and their journey had become more treacherous than they had ever imagined.

Christine spoke softly, her voice filled with concern. "We can't afford to stay here for too long. Our food and water are running out, and we have no idea how much further we have to climb."

Alex nodded in agreement. "I know, but we can't leave Celine behind. We have to ensure she's well enough to continue."

They gave Celine the last of their food and water, nourishing her as best they could. The Enchanted Forest's mysterious bounty had sustained them, but it had also led them to their current predicament. They were at a critical juncture in their quest, and they couldn't afford to falter.

As they sat by Celine's side, they could see the toll that the climb had taken on her. Her face was pale, and dark circles marred the skin beneath her closed eyes. The Enchanted Mountain had tested their endurance, and Celine had borne the brunt of it.

The forest's magic seemed to watch over them, its shadows and whispers a constant presence. It was a place of both beauty and peril, and the trio knew they had to be cautious.

With Celine resting, the exhaustion they all felt began to catch up with them. The journey had been relentless, and the Enchanted Forest had thrown challenge after challenge their way.

As the sun dipped below the horizon and the forest came alive with the songs of its mystical inhabitants, Christine and Alex made the difficult decision to rest. They lay down on the uneven ground, their bodies aching, and their hearts heavy with the knowledge that their world's fate rested on their shoulders.

The Enchanted Mountain loomed above, its peak obscured by the veil of mist. The stolen Gem of Life awaited them there, and the queen's grip on their world grew tighter with each passing moment.

With Celine by their side, they closed their eyes and surrendered to the embrace of slumber, hoping that the rest would rekindle their strength and determination for the challenges that lay ahead.

As the trio slept on the slopes of the Enchanted Mountain, they were suddenly roused from their dreams by a series of curious and powerful sounds. The forest around them seemed to come to life in an extraordinary way.

Celine, Christine, and Alex blinked their eyes open, trying to comprehend the surreal sight that met them. Before them stood a pair of unlikely companions—a majestic gray wolf and a massive brown bear. These creatures were unlike any they had ever seen, and yet they exuded an air of intelligence and purpose.

The wolf, its eyes bright with a glint of wisdom, regarded them with a steady gaze. The bear, with its towering form and a presence that felt both formidable and gentle, seemed to radiate a sense of guardianship.

Christine and Alex exchanged startled glances, their hearts pounding with a mix of fear and wonder. Celine, still weak from her earlier ordeal, tried to sit up but was met with a wave of dizziness.

The wolf, in a display of unexpected gentleness, approached Celine and nuzzled her gently. It was as if the creature sensed her vulnerability and sought to offer comfort.

The bear, meanwhile, stood sentry over the group, its eyes scanning their surroundings for any potential threats.

Christine, her voice filled with a mixture of awe and gratitude, said, "It's as if the forest has sent its protectors to watch over us."

Alex, ever the logical one, remained cautious. "We don't know these creatures' intentions, but for now, they seem to be keeping us safe."

The wolf and bear continued to stand guard, their presence a reassuring one in the midst of the unpredictable Enchanted Forest.

With newfound companions, albeit of the wild variety, Celine, Christine, and Alex settled back down, their senses alert to the sounds of the forest and the presence of their unexpected protectors. The journey had taken yet another unexpected turn, and the Enchanted Mountain still loomed above, its secrets and challenges waiting to be revealed.

With the dawn breaking over the Enchanted Mountain, the companionship of the wolf and bear took an unexpected turn. These enigmatic creatures, whose presence had offered protection and comfort, appeared to have more in store for Celine, Christine, and Alex.

As the trio watched in awe, the wolf and bear approached them, their eyes filled with a sense of purpose. The wolf nudged Celine, and the bear gestured for Christine and Alex to climb onto its broad back.

The message was clear—these creatures were inviting them to ride.

With a mixture of excitement and trepidation, Celine, Christine, and Alex accepted the unique mode of transportation. They climbed onto the bear's back, holding onto its fur for stability. The wolf took a position beside Celine, offering silent companionship.

And then, as if responding to an unspoken command, the wolf and bear began to move. With powerful grace, they carried their human companions uphill, their footsteps sure and confident on the steep and challenging terrain.

The trio marvelled at the stunning landscape that passed them by. The Enchanted Mountain was a place of breathtaking beauty, with lush flora and shimmering streams. The forest's magic was evident in every rustling leaf and murmuring brook.

Celine, who had been weakened by her earlier ordeal, now felt a renewed sense of strength as the wolf's presence beside her seemed to infuse her with vitality. Christine and Alex, riding the bear, exchanged glances filled with wonder at the incredible turn of events.

The journey became a surreal blend of the wild and the magical. The wolf and bear, with their knowing eyes and guiding instincts, led them toward the summit of the Enchanted Mountain. The stolen Gem of Life awaited, and the queen's shadow loomed ever larger.

With their unlikely companions by their side, Celine, Christine, and Alex continued their ascent. The challenges they faced on this journey were unlike any they had ever known, and they had come to accept that the Enchanted Forest held both beauty and peril.

As they ventured closer to their goal, the trio couldn't help but wonder what awaited them at the summit. The stolen gem was their only hope to save their world, and the wolf and bear were their steadfast guides on this extraordinary quest.

As the sun dipped below the horizon, painting the sky in hues of deep orange and crimson, the wolf and bear carried Celine, Christine, and Alex to the very summit of the Enchanted Mountain. They had reached their destination, the pinnacle of their arduous journey, just as the clock struck midnight.

At the stroke of midnight, an ethereal green light began to emanate from a distant point on the summit. It glowed softly, illuminating the surrounding landscape and casting a mesmerizing, otherworldly radiance.

The trio gazed in wonder at the source of the green light. It was a sight beyond imagination, a beacon that called to them like a guiding star.

Celine, her eyes filled with awe, said in a hushed voice, "That light... It must be the gem. It has to be."

Christine nodded in agreement, her heart pounding with anticipation. "We've come so far, and we're finally here, at the summit. Our world's last hope is within reach."

Alex, always the analytical one, observed, "But the queen and Asena won't make it easy for us. We need to be prepared for anything."

The wolf and bear, having carried them to their destination, now stood as silent sentinels nearby. Their role as guardians and guides seemed far from over, and the trio couldn't help but feel a deep sense of gratitude for their newfound animal companions.

With the gem shining brightly in the distance, Celine, Christine, and Alex took a moment to appreciate the beauty of the Enchanted Mountain at this extraordinary hour. The moon hung high in the sky, bathing the landscape in a gentle, silver light. The night was filled with the sounds of the forest, a chorus of unseen creatures that serenaded them with their mystical songs.

The air was crisp and invigorating, carrying with it the scents of pine and earth. They could see the outlines of ancient trees, their branches reaching out like ancient guardians of the mountain.

Celine marvelled at the stars that peppered the midnight sky, their brilliance only matched by the glow of the gem in the distance. She felt a profound connection to the Enchanted Forest, a place of wonder and enchantment, and her heart swelled with gratitude for the journey they had undertaken.

Christine's eyes were drawn to the delicate dance of fireflies that filled the night with their soft, flickering lights. The Enchanted Mountain seemed to be alive with magic, and the beauty of the moment filled her with a sense of wonder.

Alex, who had always been the tech-savvy one, found himself entranced by the natural world that surrounded them. The Enchanted Forest had shown them a different side of life, a side that couldn't be measured in lines of code or data.

In this extraordinary moment, the trio stood at the summit of the Enchanted Mountain, with the stolen Gem of Life beckoning them from afar. The queen's shadow loomed over their world, but they were filled with hope and determination.

They had faced challenges beyond their wildest dreams, forged unlikely alliances, and navigated a world that defied logic. And now, as they stood together, admiring the beauty of the Enchanted Mountain at the stroke of midnight, they knew that the final, most significant challenge awaited them.

The green light of the gem pulsed in the distance, a symbol of hope that shone brighter than any star in the night sky.

With the green light of the gem guiding them from a distance, Celine, Christine, and Alex left the summit of the Enchanted Mountain and embarked on the next leg of their quest. They descended from the peak and found themselves at the edge of a massive mist that obscured their path forward.

The mist was like a dense wall of fog, an ethereal curtain that separated them from the unknown. It was a formidable barrier, and they knew that venturing into it would be no ordinary experience.

Christine consulted the ancient book, her fingers tracing the words written on its pages. "The book says that we must cross through this mist, but it's not just any mist. It's a place where our worst feelings and fears may manifest."

Alex, always pragmatic, nodded in understanding. "So, it's like a ride through our deepest anxieties and regrets."

Celine, who had faced her own fears and doubts throughout the journey, took a deep breath. "We've come this far together, and we won't let this mist deter us. We have to cross through it to reach the gem."

As they approached the mist, they couldn't help but feel a chill in the air. It was as if the Enchanted Forest itself was trying to dissuade them from continuing. The eerie mist concealed what lay within, and the trio knew they were about to embark on a harrowing experience.

The wolf and bear, who had been their steadfast companions, remained at the edge of the mist. They exchanged knowing glances with Celine, Christine, and Alex. It was clear that the animals couldn't or wouldn't follow them into the mist, leaving the trio to face this challenge alone.

With determination in their hearts, they entered the mist, their footsteps carrying them into the unknown. The world around them transformed into a surreal and haunting landscape.

Within the mist, they encountered their deepest fears and regrets, manifestations of their own inner demons. Phantoms and Specters of their past haunted them, and the mist seemed to feed on their darkest emotions.

Christine, grappling with her fear of failure, saw herself as a child, abandoned and alone. Celine faced her insecurities, witnessing a version of herself who had never found her place in the world. Alex, confronting his own self-doubt, saw a vision of a future where his skills had become obsolete.

As they navigated through this emotional maelstrom, they supported one another, offering words of encouragement and strength. The mist was relentless, but their bond as friends was unbreakable.

The mist seemed to stretch on endlessly, a never-ending ride through their deepest vulnerabilities and fears. It was a relentless test of their resolve and determination.

As they finally began to emerge from the mist, they found themselves at the other side, shaken but still standing. The green light of the gem beckoned to them from a short distance away, and the eerie mist faded into the background.

The wolf and bear, who had remained at the edge of the mist, now approached them with a sense of quiet approval. It was as if they had passed a crucial test, proving their resilience and strength.

With the gem still glowing brightly, their journey continued. The Enchanted Forest had tested them in ways they could have never imagined, but they were determined to see it through to the end.

The trio entered the nightmarish abyss, a place where reality and illusion intertwined in a disorienting dance. As they took their first steps, the atmosphere weighed heavy on them, an oppressive shroud of despair.

In this surreal and unsettling space, the illusions took form, echoing the trio's deepest fears and insecurities. Celine, who had battled self-doubt her entire life, encountered a vision of her younger self, alone and abandoned. The illusion's cruel whispers reinforced her feelings of unworthiness, and the weight of her insecurities bore down upon her, threatening to crush her spirit.

Christine, grappling with her fear of failure, found herself surrounded by a crowd of disappointed faces, their disapproval tangible and deafening. The echoes of her perceived inadequacies reverberated through the illusion, intensifying her inner dread. Her tears mixed with the illusionary faces that judged her, and she couldn't hold back her sobs.

As Christine wept, her cries reverberated through the surreal landscape, a painful reflection of her inner turmoil. The voices of parents, long gone but forever etched in her heart, seemed to fill the air, their loving words and expectations merging into a haunting chorus.

Alex, burdened by the relentless pressure to be perfect, was thrust into a future where his skills had become obsolete. He watched in agony as his creations crumbled, leaving him feeling like a failure in a world that had moved on. The weight of his perceived inadequacies pressed down on him, and he too struggled to hold back tears.

The illusions were unrelenting, their whispers filled with self-loathing, regret, and despair. The trio was overwhelmed by the oppressive weight of the illusion, and it felt as if their very souls were being crushed.

As Christine's tearful eyes met Alex's, he could see the pain etched into her face. The illusions had taken a heavy toll on her, and her heart was burdened by the haunting voices of her parents.

With compassion in his voice, Alex moved closer to her, placing a reassuring hand on her shoulder. "I know, Christine, what we just faced was more challenging than anything we could have imagined. The illusions reached deep into our souls, but we can't afford to give in to despair. Our world is counting on us, and we've already come so far. We have to keep moving forward."

Christine sniffled and nodded, her tears still glistening in her eyes. She wiped them away with the back of her hand, her resolve slowly returning. The support of her friends and Alex's motivational words were like a beacon in the darkness, guiding her out of the depths of her own despair.

Celine, standing beside them, also offered a reassuring smile. "He's right, Christine. We've faced our deepest fears together, and we've emerged stronger each time. We can do this, as long as we're together."

With newfound determination, they collectively turned their gaze back to the distant, beckoning green light of the gem. The path ahead remained uncertain, and the challenges they would encounter were still shrouded in mystery, but they knew one thing for certain: they would face them as a united front, their friendship their most potent weapon against the trials that lay ahead.

As the trio resumed their journey through the Enchanted Forest, they soon found themselves surrounded by a disconcerting array of figures. The surreal landscape appeared to shape-shift into the familiar forms of their loved ones — parents, pets, and friends, all intermingled in an ever-changing tapestry of faces and voices.

Celine, her voice trembling, said, "Are those... our parents?"

Christine, her eyes filled with both sorrow and confusion, replied, "I think so... and look, there's my dog. I've missed him so much."

Alex, his brows furrowed as he recognized the spectral figures, added, "I see some of my old friends from school too. This is surreal."

The presence of these spectral figures sent ripples of unease through their minds. It was as if the very fabric of their reality was unravelling, each illusion a painful reminder of the bonds they held dear.

Celine's heart ached as she thought she saw her parents, their loving faces contorted into expressions of disappointment. Her pet cat, now ethereal, flickered in and out of existence, leaving her yearning for the comfort of its purring presence.

Christine, haunted by the vision of her parents from earlier, found herself unable to escape their watchful gaze. Her loyal dog, long since passed, appeared before her, and she could almost feel the warmth of its furry presence.

Alex's concentration wavered as he caught fleeting glimpses of his childhood friends and mentors. Their voices echoed through the illusion, mingling with the sounds of encouragement and doubt.

The figures, once sources of solace and companionship, now served as distractions, threatening to pull the trio deeper into the labyrinth of their own minds. It became increasingly challenging to focus on the path ahead, and the weight of their emotions made each step heavier than the last.

Despite the illusion's attempts to weaken their resolve, the trio clung to their shared determination and the unwavering bond they had forged. They whispered words of encouragement to one another, reminding themselves of the gem's importance and the destiny that lay before them.

With gritted teeth and hearts filled with conviction, they pressed forward, determined to overcome this new challenge and continue their journey deeper into the Enchanted Forest.

The mist that shrouded the trio in its enigmatic embrace was thick and unrelenting, altering their perception and separating them from one another. The forest's familiar contours were distorted, and their vision was reduced to a disorienting haze.

"Celine?" Christine's voice quivered as she called out, anxiety saturating her words. "Alex, where are you? I can't see a thing, and it feels like I'm all alone in this."

Celine's voice held both concern and determination as she responded, "Christine, I'm here with you, but it's as if the mist has stolen our senses. Alex, can you hear us? Are you alright?"

Through the mist's veil, Alex's voice sounded, "I can hear you both, but the fog is dense, and I've lost sight of you. Let's not panic. We've been through so much together, and we'll find a way back to each other."

The separation was disconcerting. Without visual cues, their world became a disorienting labyrinth, and their sense of direction was compromised. Yet, their voices, still filled with trust and resilience, became their lifelines.

In this moment, where they were deprived of sight, the strength of their friendship became more apparent than ever. Their words wove a connection that was unbreakable, transcending the mist's illusion and echoing through the labyrinth.

They took each step cautiously, the rhythm of their dialogue guiding their path. With every word, they reaffirmed their bond, reminding themselves of the importance of their quest and the collective strength that had carried them through countless trials.

As they moved forward, voices transformed into more than just communication; they were a testament to their enduring friendship, a guiding force that would ultimately lead them out of the enigmatic maze of the Enchanted Forest.

As Celine ventured further into the mist-shrouded forest, her surroundings shifted, and she found herself immersed in her deepest fears. A vivid illusion materialized before her, and it was a reflection of the greatest challenge she had ever faced - a towering, impassable wall.

This wall represented the insurmountable barriers she had encountered in her life, the moments when she had felt overwhelmed and powerless. The vivid, lifelike illusion taunted her, reminding her of the times she had faltered.

But the illusions didn't stop at her own fears. They also took on the appearance of her dearest friends, and they seemed to cry out for her help. The faces of Christine and Alex, distorted by despair, appeared as if they were trapped, their hands outstretched, pleading for assistance.

Celine's heart ached as she stood before the towering, symbolic wall, caught between her own fears and the illusions of her friends. Doubt gnawed at her, and she questioned her ability to overcome this seemingly insurmountable obstacle.

The weight of her past struggles and the desperate cries of her friends made it nearly impossible for her to move forward. She felt paralyzed by a sense of helplessness, the fog around her thickening with her despair.

From a distance, Christine's voice reached her ears, filled with concern. "Celine, where are you? Are you okay?"

Celine, her voice shaky, replied, "I... I can't move. I'm stuck in front of this wall. And I can see you and Alex, but you both look so lost."

Alex chimed in, "We're here for you, Celine. You've helped us through so much. You can do this."

But Celine's inner struggle was far from over. The illusions of her friends and the imposing wall still seemed insurmountable. In this moment of vulnerability, she grappled with her fears, desperately seeking a way to overcome the obstacles that threatened to derail their journey.

As Alex moved through the mist-enveloped forest, the eerie illusions began to take form around him, and he was faced with his most profound challenge. Before him stood a colossal, intricate maze, an intricate web of winding paths that seemed impossible to navigate.

This maze symbolized the labyrinth of choices and decisions he had encountered throughout his life. The complexities of his own mind, the paths he had taken, and the ones he had left behind all manifested before him in this surreal illusion.

But the illusions didn't stop at his personal challenges. They also took on the visage of his friends, Christine and Celine. They appeared distraught, wandering through the labyrinthine maze, their voices filled with desperation as they called out for guidance.

The weight of his past decisions and the helplessness of his friends' illusions weighed heavily on Alex. Doubt began to creep into his thoughts, and he questioned his ability to find a way out of this bewildering maze.

The illusions of his friends, distorted by the complexity of the maze, seemed to plead for his aid. They cried out for direction, their voices echoing his own sense of confusion.

Christine's voice, tinged with concern, called out to him from a distance. "Alex, where are you? Are you okay?"

Alex, his voice reflecting his struggle, responded, "I'm here, but I'm trapped in this maze. I can see you and Celine, but I don't know how to find my way out."

Celine's voice added, "You've always been the one who guides us with your clarity, Alex. Trust yourself. You can overcome this."

The complexity of the maze, the weight of his past, and the illusions of his friends created a tumultuous internal struggle. In this moment of vulnerability, Alex faced his greatest challenge, wrestling with the choices and paths that had led him to this critical juncture.

As Christine journeyed deeper into the enigmatic mist, the illusions around her began to take shape, revealing her most profound challenge. Before her stood a towering, dark forest, dense and forbidding, with trees so tightly intertwined that they formed an impassable barrier.

This ominous forest represented the isolation and self-imposed barriers she had grappled with throughout her life. It was a symbol of her fear of being alone, of closing herself off from the world, and of the moments when she had been unable to break free from her own solitude.

Yet the illusions didn't end with her own challenges. They also took on the form of her dearest friends, Celine and Alex. Their forms appeared trapped within the tangled undergrowth, their voices filled with a yearning for connection and guidance.

The weight of her own fears and the despair of her friends' illusions pressed heavily upon Christine's heart. It became increasingly difficult for her to take even a single step forward, as she grappled with the suffocating isolation of the illusion.

From a distance, Celine's voice called out, filled with concern. "Christine, where are you? We're here for you."

Christine, her voice trembling with vulnerability, replied, "I'm surrounded by this oppressive forest, and I can see both of you, but it's as though you're trapped in it. I can't move forward."

Alex's voice chimed in, "You're never alone, Christine. We've always been there for each other. Believe in our bond."

Christine's internal struggle was far from over. The oppressive forest and the weight of her own isolation, combined with the yearning of her friends' illusions for connection, created a storm of emotions that threatened to engulf her. In this moment of vulnerability, she was forced to confront her deepest fears, searching for a way to break free from the stifling embrace of the illusion.

As Celine stood before the imposing wall of her greatest fears and the illusions of her friends, a revelation began to take shape in her mind. She realized that the key to moving forward lay not in collectively overcoming these challenges but in each of them individually confronting their fears.

A sense of determination surged within her, and she called out to her friends through the mist. "Christine, Alex, I've realized something. We each have to face our own challenges and illusions individually. Only by conquering our deepest fears can we find the path forward."

Christine's voice carried a mix of understanding and encouragement. "Celine, you're right. We can't rely on each other to overcome what's holding us back. We have to find the strength within ourselves."

Alex, in agreement, added, "We've always been there for each other, but this time, it's about self-discovery. Let's do this."

Empowered by their shared realization, Celine, Christine, and Alex began to turn their attention inward, confronting their individual challenges and illusions with newfound resolve. The misty labyrinth might have separated them physically, but in this moment, they were united by a common purpose—to conquer their deepest fears and find their own paths forward.

As Celine grappled with her inner challenges, the haunting memories of her greatest fears and the illusions of her friends seemed to close in on her. In a moment of desperation, she found herself starting to forget, losing herself to the overwhelming illusion.

Then, a faint but familiar melody began to surface in her mind. It was the song "Titanium." The lyrics, like a lifeline, rose from her memories and filled her thoughts:

"I am titanium."

She whispered the words to herself, a mantra that had carried her through countless trials in the past. But as she sang those words, a transformation began to unfold. Her voice grew louder, her tone more resolute.

"I am titanium!"

With each utterance of the lyrics, the illusionary obstacles around her began to shatter. The imposing wall of her deepest fears crumbled into nothingness, and the illusions of her friends dissolved into the mist.

In the wake of her resounding declaration, the mist itself started to part, unveiling a brilliant green light in the distance. It called to her, drawing her in with an irresistible allure.

Celine, no longer confined by her inner fears, stepped forward, following the beckoning green light. It illuminated her path, casting aside the illusions that had once held her captive. With each step, she moved closer to the source of the light, a newfound sense of purpose guiding her way.

Christine, surrounded by her internal struggles and the illusions of her friends, felt a profound connection to the power of stories and the wisdom they held. She thought of the books that had shaped her world, especially a quote from a beloved tale:

"We've all got both light and dark inside us. What matters is the part we choose to act on. That's who we really are."

As she spoke these words aloud, a transformation occurred. The illusions that had bound her and her friends began to dissipate, their forms fading into the mist. The weight of her own solitude and isolation lifted, and she found herself free of the all-encompassing forest.

With a newfound sense of clarity, she saw a magnificent, ethereal whale in the distance. The whale moved with grace and purpose, and it seemed to invite her to follow. Christine was drawn to its majestic presence, understanding that it was a symbol of guidance and wisdom.

She followed the whale, its gentle movements leading her toward a radiant green light that shone like a beacon. As she drew nearer to the source of the light, the mist and illusions continued to recede, clearing her path.

Finally, when she reached the source of the light, she discovered Celine waiting there. Overwhelmed by relief, she rushed forward and embraced her dear friend. In this moment, they found solace in each other's presence and in the newfound strength that had carried them through their individual trials.

Alex, battling the disorienting illusions and the weight of his own fears and memories, began to feel a profound dizziness that threatened to overwhelm him. Tears welled up in his eyes as he was immersed in the darkest recollections of his past.

The memories he faced were some of the most painful, and they threatened to consume him. He could barely stand, his vision blurred by the tears that streamed down his face. Yet, amid the turmoil, a flicker of a forgotten algorithm surfaced in his mind. It was one he had once created, a tale about a tortoise and a hare.

In his moment of desperation, he uttered the words, "If a hare can be seen by a tortoise, why can't I?" The utterance rang out, a declaration of his determination to break free from the illusionary web that ensnared him.

With that cry, the illusions around him dissolved, and the daunting memories that had haunted him vanished. However, one figure remained—the faint, spectral silhouette of his mother. She had left him when he was only four months old, a painful absence that still lingered in his heart.

Alex couldn't help but shed tears for the mother he had never truly known, the silent figure serving as a haunting reminder. But, with a heavy heart, he wiped away his tears, summoning a reservoir of inner strength.

Singing the words from "Titanium," his voice quivered but grew stronger with each verse:

"I'm bulletproof, nothing to lose Fire away, fire away Ricochet, you take your aim Fire away, fire away."

As he continued to walk, he noticed a faint, guiding presence—a spectral figure that resembled his mother. Following her lead, he made his way toward the radiant green light.

As Alex made his way toward the radiant green light, he was drawn closer to the presence of his spectral mother, a figure he had longed for, yet could never truly reach. His tears flowed freely as he followed her ethereal form, guided by a longing that had been buried deep within him.

With each step, the weight of his past and the emotions he had carried for years bore down on him. The reunion with his mother's spectral presence evoked a profound sorrow, and he wept openly, mourning the absence he had felt throughout his life.

Christine and Celine, having already conquered their own challenges, watched as Alex's emotions flowed. The distance that had once separated them now seemed inconsequential, and they rushed to his side, their hearts heavy with empathy.

In a moment of intense emotion, the three friends embraced, their tears merging into a shared catharsis. The reunion was more than physical; it was a convergence of their individual journeys, a testament to the unbreakable bond they shared.

Alex's sobs were met with words of solace and understanding from his friends. They whispered assurances that he was not alone, that they would face whatever challenges lay ahead together, and that the strength of their friendship would see them through.

The moment held an emotional weight that transcended words, an unspoken promise that they would support and uplift each other, no matter the trials they faced. In the unity of their embrace, they found the resolve to confront the mysteries of the Enchanted Forest and the gem that held the fate of their world.

With their tears of reunion slowly drying, Celine took a step closer to Alex. She could sense the lingering weight of his emotions, the memories that had resurfaced, and the complex feelings he grappled with regarding his mother's absence.

In a gentle, comforting voice, she said, "Alex, you've shown incredible strength, and we're here for you. We're a team, and we'll face whatever comes our way, together."

Alex nodded, grateful for her understanding and the unwavering support of his friends. The bond they shared had only grown stronger through the trials they had endured in the Enchanted Forest.

With a collective determination, they resumed their journey, walking side by side. The radiant green light beckoned them forward, a symbol of the hope and purpose that had carried them this far.

As they ventured deeper into the heart of the forest, their steps were imbued with a newfound resolve. They knew that the challenges ahead might be just as formidable as those they had faced within the abyss of the mind, but they were no longer afraid.

United by their unbreakable bond and the strength they had found within themselves, they were ready to confront whatever mysteries and obstacles the Enchanted Forest had in store.

CHAPTER 6

The Final Game

* this is the location where this scene is set and this chapter has some pics:)

The trio, having emerged from the depths of their inner challenges, now stood before a weathered and ancient bridge that spanned a churning river. It was a bridge of unknown origins, its timeworn planks and rusted ironwork revealing the countless years it had withstood. With no alternative path before them, they ventured onto the bridge.

As they took their initial steps, the bridge emitted eerie creaking and groaning sounds. Each footfall seemed to reverberate through the timeworn wood, causing the bridge to sway slightly. It was as if the old structure was awakened from a deep slumber, and it voiced its protests against the intruders.

Despite the unsettling sounds, the three friends pressed forward, determination guiding their every step. The bridge was the only route across the river, and the mysteries of the Enchanted Forest beckoned them onward.

With every creak and sway, they continued their cautious journey, their eyes fixed on the horizon, and their hearts steeled for whatever challenges the bridge and the forest beyond might present.

As the friends advanced along the rickety bridge, eerie sounds began to echo through the forest. The once quiet surroundings transformed into a nightmarish symphony of slithering and thunderous footfalls. It was then that the source of their terror emerged from the shadows.

Hissing serpents slithered from the underbrush, their eyes gleaming with malice, while a chorus of low growls signalled the approach of massive gorillas. The forest itself had come alive, its formidable guardians summoned to defend its secrets.

Panicked and gasping for breath, the three friends pushed forward, desperation guiding their steps. Celine's voice trembled as she shouted, "We have to keep moving! There's no turning back now!"

The snakes, venomous fangs bared, lunged at them with deadly precision, while the gorillas, their enormous bodies rippling with strength, blocked their path. Alex's heart raced as he yelled, "Stay together! We'll find a way out of this!"

Their escape led them to a towering tree with branches that seemed to stretch into eternity. At its peak, a colossal python hung like a sinister omen. Christine's voice quivered with fear as she said, "We have no choice. We need to climb the tree to escape."

The python struck with lightning speed, attempting to ensnare them in its lethal coils. They fought with all their might, struggling to break free, leaving the snake hissing in frustration.

Despite their harrowing escape, they faced a new ordeal. A branch jutting out from the bridge was infested with red ants, their fiery bites inflicting unbearable pain. Christine gasped, "We can't stay here. We have to jump."

Alex, his voice filled with determination, urged them on, "We'll find another way, but not here."

With a shared understanding, they made a daring leap from the bridge, descending into the river below. The forest's enigmatic challenges were far from over, but they were determined to press on, driven by the hope of recovering the gem of life and saving their world.

Their plunge into the river was a desperate escape, a leap of faith to evade the relentless horrors of the bridge. But as they hit the water, a torrential current threatened to pull them under. They struggled to stay afloat, their limbs growing heavy with exhaustion. In the churning river, their minds swirled with confusion and fear, and once again, they were subjected to nightmarish visions.

Their surroundings dissolved into a haunting dreamscape. In the dream, they witnessed their own deaths, each vision more chilling than the last. The relentless onslaught of these visions threatened to consume them, as if the river itself sought to claim them for its own.

Just as it seemed they might succumb to the river's relentless grip, they were wrenched from the water and deposited onto the riverbank. Gasping for breath and shivering from the cold, they found themselves in a new landscape—a dense, primeval forest.

The forest was unlike anything they had encountered before. Towering trees loomed overhead, their branches forming a natural canopy that cast the world below in shadow. A thick underbrush of vibrant green foliage and mysterious, fragrant flowers stretched out in every direction.

The air was heavy with an otherworldly humidity, and the sounds of the forest were an enchanting cacophony of birdcalls, insects, and distant waterfalls. The forest felt alive, as if it possessed its own consciousness, observing their every move.

As they navigated through the dense foliage, the mysteries of this new environment unfolded around them. What secrets did the forest hold, and how would its enigmatic nature challenge them on their quest to find the gem of life?

Amid the lush, enigmatic forest, the friends sought solace under the comforting shade of a giant tree. Here, sheltered from the sun-dappled mysteries of their surroundings, they opened the ancient book, its pages whispering secrets and guiding them onward.

Within its timeworn pages, they found a cryptic message. It read: "The path to the castle shall be revealed, but first, wild physical fears must be faced. Beyond the forest's heart, where shadows cast their spell, your courage shall be tested, and your destiny, unveiled."

As they contemplated the riddle, Alex's voice broke the silence. "The forest's heart—could it be the deepest, darkest part of this place?"

Celine nodded, her eyes filled with determination. "Whatever challenges lie ahead, we'll face them together. Our bond is our strength."

Christine agreed, her voice resolute. "And our motivation is our compass. We carry the hopes of our world with us."

With newfound determination and the weight of their mission pressing upon them, they set forth into the heart of the forest, where unknown physical fears awaited. The forest seemed to come alive, the very trees whispering secrets of the trials to come.

As they ventured deeper, the shadows grew denser, and the air was laden with a palpable sense of anticipation. The friends shared stories and laughter, their words forging a bridge over the uncharted waters of the unknown.

Together, they braved the challenges that lay ahead, knowing that their courage would be their greatest ally on the path to the castle and the ultimate showdown with Asena, the villainous queen who held the gem of life.

As the trio ventured deeper into the forest's heart, they soon encountered a challenge as bizarre as it was relentless. A cloud of mosquitoes, a voracious swarm, descended upon them. The incessant buzzing and painful bites left them in a frenzied panic.

Christine, quick on her feet, remembered the lighter she had tucked away in her backpack. With a determined glint in her eye, she ignited a nearby branch and conjured a makeshift torch. The flames flickered to life, casting an eerie glow against the surrounding darkness.

With the burning branch held high, she waved it frantically, causing the mosquitoes to scatter in disarray. The pests recoiled from the flames and the trio's valiant stand. Soon, they found themselves free from the relentless torment, surrounded only by the fading embers of their makeshift torch.

In the aftermath of the mosquito onslaught, they caught their breath, their faces streaked with sweat and determination. The forest had thrown a test of endurance and ingenuity their way, and they had risen to the occasion, yet again.

Their unwavering spirit persisted, knowing that the path to the castle held further challenges, each designed to test their resolve and courage. The gem of life remained the ultimate prize, and they were determined to secure it, no matter the cost.

Before them loomed an imposing set of colossal trees, their thick trunks standing like sentinels guarding an uncharted territory. At the heart of this enigmatic grove, a series of slender ropes dangled like tantalizing threads leading to the unknown. The friends realized they needed to swing through this arboreal maze to continue their journey.

Celine, her adventurous spirit still burning bright, volunteered to go first. She approached the rope, grabbed hold, and with a leap, swung gracefully from one tree to another, her laughter ringing through the forest.

Christine followed suit, her bookworm tendencies momentarily cast aside as she embraced the thrill of the swing. With determined resolve, she propelled herself through the air, landing safely on the far side.

Alex, however, was less eager to undertake this daring feat. His reluctance was palpable, and he clung to the notion of solid ground like a true tech enthusiast. "You know I'm not cut out for this, right?" he mumbled, palms sweaty as he eyed the rope with uncertainty.

Celine couldn't resist a teasing grin. "Come on, Alex! It's just like coding, but with more gravity involved."

With their encouragement, Alex took a deep breath and summoned his inner adventurer. He gripped the rope tightly, his knuckles turning white, and then, with a mix of trepidation and determination, he flung himself into the air.

he screamed from the top of his throat which sounded like a gorilla who is in labour

The ensuing spectacle was nothing short of comical, as he dangled from the rope, arms and legs flailing, his face a mixture of terror and exhilaration. The girls couldn't help but burst into fits of laughter as they watched their friend's reluctant yet hilarious swing.

Finally, after what felt like an eternity, Alex reached the other side, his relief palpable. The friends had successfully conquered the forest's whimsical rope challenge, and they were one step closer to their ultimate goal.

The friends' journey through the mystical forest took a perilous turn when they stumbled upon a pack of menacing wolves. The predatory glint in their eyes sent shivers down their spines, and terror gripped their hearts.

They fled through the forest, tears of desperation streaming down their faces. It seemed as though their perilous escape was futile, as the wolves relentlessly closed in, herding them into a hopeless corner. The situation appeared dire.

Celine, her voice trembling, gasped, "We can't let them catch us! Keep running!" Christine, her breath ragged, cried out, "I can't believe it's come to this! We can't give up!"

Alex, his face etched with determination, urged, "Keep moving, guys! We'll find a way out of this!"

Just when it seemed their fate was sealed, two lone wolves, their fur shimmering with an otherworldly luminescence, emerged from the shadows. They growled with authority and confidence, and the other wolves, as if bound by an unspoken pact, bowed in deference.

The friends watched in awe as the pack of wolves that had cornered them retreated, leaving them untouched and unharmed. The two saviours stood guard until the others had retreated completely, and then, with a final, enigmatic glance, they too disappeared into the forest.

The trio exchanged incredulous glances, their minds racing to comprehend the astonishing turn of events. Could it be that their destiny was intertwined with the very essence of this mystical realm?

Eager to unravel the enigma, they turned to the ancient book, which had guided them through countless trials. Its pages revealed the astonishing truth. Every creature in the forest, every sentient being, bore witness to their journey. They were not mere intruders; they were the heroes of a legend, foretold to restore balance to their world.

The weight of this revelation settled upon their shoulders, and they continued their quest with a newfound sense of purpose. The mystical forest was their ally, and their destiny was inexorably entwined with the fate of their world.

As the friends pressed onward, their footsteps light and conversation animated, they couldn't help but reflect on the strange and often perilous trials they'd faced one after another. The mystical forest had tested their courage, wits, and bonds, but they had grown stronger with each challenge they surmounted.

Celine spoke up, her voice tinged with both wonder and trepidation. "Isn't it incredible how we've managed to overcome every obstacle so far? It's almost as if the forest is guiding us."

Christine nodded in agreement. "Yes, it's as if the forest itself is on our side, helping us fulfill our destiny."

Alex chimed in, "Well, whatever the reason, I'm just glad we have each other to rely on."

Their discussion was abruptly interrupted when they stumbled upon a familiar sight—a basket filled with food, just like the one they had discovered earlier. Famished from their journey and lulled into a false sense of security by their previous successes, they eagerly devoured its contents.

Celine savoured a bite of fruit, then smiled and remarked, "You know, aside from a few close calls, we haven't faced as much trouble as we expected."

Christine, her cheeks flushed with embarrassment, nodded. "It's almost as if we're being led through a carefully designed path."

Just as Alex was about to voice his own thoughts, a deep, bone-chilling growl erupted from the shadows. Their gazes snapped toward the source, and their hearts sank as they came face to face with a majestic but imposing lion, its golden eyes fixed upon them.

The forest had once again thrown a test their way, a ferocious predator challenging their very survival. This time, they couldn't help but wonder if their previous successes had only been preludes to the true test that lay ahead.

The lion, a magnificent and powerful beast, surged forward with a ferocity that sent shivers down their spines. Its thunderous roars echoed through the forest, urging them to sprint faster, each footfall pounding against the forest floor.

Celine's voice trembled with urgency as she shouted, "We need to find an escape route, fast!"

Christine's eyes scanned their surroundings, and she spotted a narrow path veering to their right. "There! Let's take that path. Maybe it'll lead us to safety."

Without hesitation, they followed her lead, sprinting down the narrow path as the lion's relentless pursuit bore down upon them. The path seemed to stretch on forever, the tension in the air palpable as they raced toward an uncertain destination.

Then, the path came to an abrupt halt at a towering wall bristling with cement spikes. Their faces paled as they realized the challenge before them. They would have to jump through the wall, a feat that seemed daunting, even insurmountable.

Alex's voice quivered with anxiety. "This is insane! Are we really going to do this?"

Christine clenched her teeth, her eyes fixed on the wall ahead. "We don't have a choice, Alex. It's either this or the lion."

Celine's resolve shone in her eyes. "On three, everyone! One... two... three!"

As they shouted in unison, they hurled themselves toward the menacing wall, cements spikes appearing to loom ever closer. Their hearts raced in unison with their collective cry, and for a split second, it felt as though time had stopped.

But they made it through, narrowly evading the spikes that seemed destined to pierce them. As they tumbled to the other side, their hearts raced, adrenaline surging through their veins. Their shouts of triumph echoed through the forest, a testament to their unyielding determination and the unbreakable bond that had carried them through each daunting challenge.

As they landed on the other side of the wall of cement spikes, Celine and Christine couldn't hold back their laughter. Their giggles rang through the forest, echoing off the towering trees.

Celine pointed at Alex, who was blushing brighter than a ripe tomato. "Alex, this forest adventure is turning you into a fashion icon! Your pants, or what's left of them, are the latest forest chic trend!"

Christine chimed in, her laughter infectious. "You've heard of fashionably late, but you, my friend, are fashionably torn!"

Alex's face was a deep shade of crimson as he realized the state of his pants. With haste, he darted behind a nearby tree, muttering under his breath about the unfairness of forest fashion shows.

Celine couldn't resist teasing further. "Well, you've certainly given the wildlife a show, Alex! Bravo!"

Christine added with a grin, "I think the forest critters are considering you for a cameo in their next 'Best-Dressed Human in the Forest' documentary."

Emerging from behind the tree with a fresh pair of pants, Alex couldn't help but chuckle at the hilarity of the situation. "I'll make sure to wear jeans next time. They seem more lion-proof."

With laughter still bubbling within them, they continued their journey. The memory of this absurd escape added a touch of levity to their adventure, reminding them that even in the most challenging moments, a good laugh could be a powerful source of strength and camaraderie.

The trio approached a formidable gate, unlike any they had encountered before. It stood tall and imposing, the sheer strength of it exuding an air of invincibility. It was firmly locked, as if daring them to discover the secrets that lay beyond.

The ancient book appeared in Celine's hands, and its pages shimmered as it conveyed a message: "Congratulations, brave adventurers! You've reached the gate that guards the path to the castle. To open it, you must prove your wits and understanding of geometry."

Christine's eyes sparkled with curiosity. "Geometry and riddles? We can handle that!"

The gate bore a series of intricate riddles etched into its surface. They read the riddles one by one and began to solve them as a team, their minds racing to find the answers.

Alex's voice echoed as he pondered, "What has keys but can't open locks?" Celine replied, "That's an interesting one. It must be a piano!"

Christine's excitement grew as she examined the next riddle. "What is as light as a feather, yet even the strongest man couldn't hold it for long?"

The answer, they realized, was "breath."

With each riddle they solved, the gate seemed to acknowledge their intelligence, its formidable presence slowly softening.

Once they'd successfully cracked all the riddles, a new challenge emerged. The book instructed them to apply their knowledge of geometry to unlock the gate.

Alex scratched his head, contemplating the geometric patterns engraved on the gate's surface. "Let's see if this triangle relates to that rectangle. Maybe we need to find the right angles and proportions."

Celine pointed at a set of lines that seemed to converge in a particular way. "I think we need to connect these points with lines that form specific shapes."

Christine chimed in, "And perhaps we should measure the angles and sides accurately to ensure they meet the geometric criteria."

With their combined knowledge and problem-solving skills, they carefully applied their understanding of geometry to the gate. As they did, the ancient lock on the gate began to click and shift. With a resonant, echoing groan, the gate slowly creaked open, revealing the path that led to the castle.

They couldn't help but exchange triumphant smiles, for they had once again overcome a challenging trial, proving their wits and determination. With the gate now open, their journey continued, taking them one step closer to their ultimate goal.

As they ventured deeper into the forest, they found themselves presented with a new challenge that was unlike any they had faced before. The ancient book bore a series of riddles, each one more intricate and enigmatic than the last. It was a test of their intellect, a labyrinth of wordplay and wit.

The first riddle:

"I'm taken from a mine, and shut up in a wooden case, from which I'm never released, and yet I am used by almost every person. What am I?"

Christine pondered for a moment before her eyes lit up. "A pencil lead! Mined graphite encased in wood."

The book glowed in agreement, confirming their correct answer.

The second riddle:

"I'm not alive, but I can grow; I don't have lungs, but I need air; I don't have a mouth, but water kills me. What am I?"

Alex was quick to respond. "Fire! It's not alive, but it 'grows' as it spreads, it needs oxygen to burn, and water extinguishes it."

The book confirmed their answer, the shimmer of success dancing in its pages.

The third riddle:

"I speak without a mouth and hear without ears. I have no body, but I come alive with the wind. What am I?"

Celine smiled as she replied, "An echo! It may not have a physical form, but it 'lives' when sound carries through the air."

The ancient book acknowledged their answer, and they continued to tackle the riddles one after another.

They worked through each riddle meticulously, solving them with a sense of unity and accomplishment.

With their final riddle deciphered, Christine noted that each riddle's answer started with the letters "P," "F," and "E," respectively. The letters spelled out "PFE," and with a glint of understanding, she combined them. "The letters we've found spell 'PFE'—now, together, let's make it count."

The three friends raised their voices in unison. "PFE!" they shouted and then blinked three times.

In a flash of radiant light, they felt a surge of energy and determination, and they knew they were one step closer to their ultimate destination. They continued their journey, their spirits high, having conquered the labyrinth of riddles and emerged victorious.

Before them stood the gate, an intricate masterpiece of steel and stone. It was locked, and the only clue they had was a directive from the ancient book: "Reflect light onto the midpoint of the gate using your knowledge of geometry."

They gazed at the gate, pondering the task ahead. It was clear that geometry held the key to opening the imposing barrier.

Alex, always the one to embrace a challenge, stepped forward with a determined look. "Geometry, my friends. Let's think angles, lines, and reflections. We need to be precise about this."

Celine nodded, her eyes focused on the gate. "We have to consider the exact angle and the direction in which we reflect the light. The midpoint is crucial."

Christine, ever the bookworm, chimed in with her idea. "What if we reflect the light at a 90-degree angle to the left? It might just be the right approach. If we place the light source just right, it could hit the midpoint."

With the gem in hand, they positioned themselves with precision. Alex meticulously adjusted the angle, ensuring that the light would strike the midpoint of the gate.

As the beam of light hit the exact spot, the gate responded with a subtle vibration. The massive doors slowly began to creak open, revealing the path beyond.

Excitement and relief washed over them. Their teamwork and their grasp of geometry had successfully unlocked the gate. They exchanged glances filled with pride and determination. They knew that the challenges ahead would grow more complex, but they were ready to face them head-on, for their destiny lay within the heart of the forest.

Their unity was their greatest strength, and they pressed forward with confidence, ready to confront whatever awaited them.

*the lion-chasing scene

CHAPTER 7

The Beginning Of The End

As they passed through the open gate, they were met with a breathtaking sight. Before them lay a lush, vibrant meadow, bathed in the soft glow of twilight. The gentle scent of blooming wildflowers filled the air, and a feeling of serenity washed over them.

And then, she appeared. Asena, the enigmatic Queen who had eluded them throughout their journey, emerged from the shadows of the forest. Her presence was no longer shrouded in mystery; she stood before them as a gracious, regal figure.

With a warm smile, Asena extended her hand in greeting. "Welcome, brave travellers. I am Asena, and it is an honour to meet you."

The three friends exchanged glances, the weight of their long and arduous journey still fresh in their minds. But there was something different about Asena, an aura of kindness that emanated from her.

Christine, always quick to trust in the goodness of people, took the first step and shook Asena's hand. "Thank you for your warm welcome, Asena. We've come a long way, and we've faced many challenges."

Celine and Alex, more cautious by nature, also extended their hands to Asena. "It's a pleasure to meet you," Alex added.

Asena's eyes twinkled with understanding. "I've watched your journey closely, and I must say, you've shown great courage and determination. You've overcome every obstacle in your path."

She gestured toward a collection of small cottages nestled at the edge of the meadow. "I invite you to stay here, to rest and rejuvenate. You've earned it. There's much to discuss, and I believe we can help each other."

The friends exchanged curious glances, uncertain of what lay ahead. But with their destinies intertwined with the enigmatic Queen Asena, they knew that the final chapters of their journey were about to unfold, and the true nature of the gem of life would be revealed.

The moment they stepped through the imposing gates of the castle, they found themselves immersed in a world of enchantment. The castle's interior was a breathtaking sight, a fusion of timeless elegance and nature's splendour.

The walls were adorned with intricate murals that seemed to come to life as the natural light filtered through ornate stained glass windows, casting a kaleidoscope of colours across the polished marble floors. Vines and ivy crept along the walls as if nature itself had reclaimed this ancient structure.

Chandeliers of glistening crystals hung from the ceilings, filling the air with a soft, ethereal glow. The air was filled with a delicate, intoxicating fragrance that could only be described as the scent of pure magic.

As they ventured deeper into the heart of the castle, they discovered lush gardens that flourished indoors, the boundaries between the outside world and the castle's interior blurred by the sheer grandeur of the place. Exotic and vibrant flowers bloomed in profusion, and small, crystal-clear streams meandered through the gardens.

The sounds of birdsong and the gentle trickle of water filled the air, and they felt as though they had entered a realm of timeless wonder. Every corner of the castle revealed a new, awe-inspiring vista, a testament to the skill and artistry of its builders.

Asena led them to a grand chamber within the castle, a room of undeniable magnificence and significance. She paused at the threshold, allowing them to take in the splendour before them.

The room was a masterpiece of both art and functionality. Tall, arched windows allowed the golden rays of the sun to flood the space, giving it an otherworldly radiance. Silk curtains in hues of sapphire and emerald billowed in the gentle breeze, their colours shimmering like the gem they had come to retrieve.

The walls were adorned with murals that depicted the entire history of the gem of life, from its creation to its theft by the villainous Queen. The scenes seemed to come alive, the figures within them moving with an ethereal grace.

In the centre of the room stood an ornate pedestal, crafted from the purest alabaster. It held a gleaming, multifaceted gem, radiating a soft, pulsating light. The gem of life, their ultimate goal, was within reach.

Asena gestured toward the gem, her eyes filled with reverence. "This is the heart of our world, the gem of life. It has been stolen, and with your help, we can restore it to its rightful place."

The room seemed to hold its breath, as though it too was waiting for their decision. The fate of their world rested in their hands, and as they approached the gem, they couldn't help but feel the weight of their destiny.

Asena excused herself from the room, leaving the three friends alone with the gem of life. She had much to contemplate, and her duties as a guardian of the gem required her attention elsewhere.

Left to their own devices, the friends gathered around the gem, their eyes fixed on its radiant core. Yet, as they stared at the gem, a lingering doubt crept into Asena's thoughts.

She made her way to a different chamber where an intricate map was etched into the stone floor. It depicted the entire world, with intricate markings and cryptic symbols that held the key to the gem's restoration.

As she studied the map, her thoughts churned with suspicion. How did these three, who had suddenly arrived in their world, possess the knowledge to restore the gem of life? The world had long believed that the gem's secret was known only to a chosen few, and that knowledge had been closely guarded for centuries.

Asena couldn't shake the feeling that there was more to these travellers than met the eye. She couldn't afford to let her guard down, even in the presence of those she had come to see as allies. The fate of the gem and their world was at stake, and she was determined to uncover the truth.

In the room with the gem of life, the three friends gathered in hushed voices, their expressions tense and determined. They knew that their mission was to restore the gem to its rightful place and save their world. But they also understood that the world they had entered was not their own, and Asena's intentions remained uncertain.

Celine, her voice barely more than a whisper, spoke her thoughts. "We can't be certain of Asena's true motives. We have to be cautious."

Christine nodded in agreement. "We've come too far to let this opportunity slip through our fingers. We need the gem, but we can't be sure if Asena is on our side."

Alex, ever the pragmatic one, laid out their plan. "We'll wait until Asena falls asleep, and then we'll make our move. We can't afford to be caught off guard."

With their plan in place, they settled in, their eyes never leaving the gem that held the key to their world's salvation. Asena's intentions remained shrouded in mystery, and they were determined to uncover the truth, even if it meant taking matters into their own hands.

As they waited for the right moment to make their move, Alex couldn't help but notice something peculiar. The room had access to electricity, and there,

hidden in a corner, was a power outlet. It seemed out of place in a world that had felt so ancient and mystical.

Curiosity got the better of him, and he reached for his smartphone, which had miraculously retained its charge throughout their journey. He plugged it into the outlet and watched in amazement as it began to charge.

Once his phone was sufficiently charged, Alex couldn't resist the temptation of exploring this new world through the lens of technology. He opened his YouTube app and began to watch a series of captivating and mesmerizing short videos.

The captivating content of YouTube shorts, filled with humour, creativity, and innovation, served as a momentary escape from the weight of their mission. For a brief period, they were transported from the enchanting yet uncertain world around them to the limitless world of the internet.

His friends exchanged bemused glances but allowed him this brief respite. In the midst of their perilous quest, a moment of distraction seemed almost necessary, a reminder of the world they had left behind.

The call for dinner echoed through the castle, and the three friends reluctantly tore their gaze away from the captivating world of YouTube shorts. They had a mission to complete, but for now, they would have to play the role of guests in Asena's enigmatic realm.

As they descended the castle's grand staircase to join Asena for dinner, Celine's demeanour shifted. Her steps became hesitant, and her expression grew distant. It was as though a sudden unease had settled over her, casting a shadow on her usual enthusiasm.

Christine and Alex exchanged concerned glances but remained silent. They couldn't deny that the world they had entered was unlike anything they had ever known, and it seemed to have a peculiar effect on each of them.

Dinner with Asena would be an opportunity to glean more information, but it would also require them to remain vigilant. The gem of life was within reach, and their world's fate hung in the balance.

Celine's unease remained a mystery, but in this enigmatic world, they had learned to trust their instincts and tread carefully.

As they settled at the dining table, Celine took her seat, her unease still lingering. The room had large, ornate windows that offered a view of the enchanting surroundings outside, a reminder of the beauty and mystery of this world.

Through the glass, her eyes widened as she caught sight of a magnificent creature. A lion, regal and powerful, stood just beyond the window. Its golden mane seemed to catch fire in the soft glow of the evening sun, and its eyes held an intelligence and intensity that transcended the ordinary.

The sight of the lion sent a shiver down her spine, and she couldn't help but wonder about the significance of this unexpected encounter. It was as though the world itself was sending her a message, a reminder of the untamed and wild nature that lay just beyond the veneer of civilization.

At that moment, it became clear to her. The pieces of the puzzle fell into place, and the truth unfolded like a tapestry. The lion had been a guiding force, a silent guardian, and the orchestrator of their trials and challenges. It had been a test of their strength, courage, and determination.

Celine's heart raced as she realized the implications of her discovery. It meant that Asena, the lion, and the mystical world they had entered were all part of a grand design. She had been a puppet in a larger scheme, and the fate of their world rested on her choices and actions.

As the pieces of the puzzle came together, Celine understood that she was not merely a traveller in this world; she was a key player in a complex game, one that would determine the destiny of the gem of life and the world it sustained.

Dinner with Asena was a grand affair. The table was adorned with a feast of exotic dishes, the likes of which they had never seen in their own world. Colourful fruits, fragrant spices, and dishes that seemed to shimmer with enchantment filled the table.

Celine, still processing her revelation, ate only a little, her appetite diminished by the weight of her newfound knowledge. Alex, on the other hand, embraced the feast with gusto, savouring the Flavors of this mysterious world. Christine, ever the cautious one, ate slowly, taking in the tastes and textures of each dish.

The conversation flowed, and Asena shared stories of her world, her role as a guardian, and the significance of the gem of life. Yet, beneath the veneer of hospitality, a tension lingered.

After a polite exchange, they bid Asena goodnight and began their ascent to the room where the gem was kept. The mysteries of this world were deepening, and the gem's power remained a tantalizing enigma.

Inside the room, the atmosphere was thick with tension. They had just returned from their dinner with Asena, and the weight of their mission pressed upon them. Celine couldn't shake the feeling that their every move was being watched, and she shared her unease with her friends.

Alex, ever the pragmatic one, tried to lighten the mood. "Did you guys notice that the food we had in the forest was remarkably similar to what we ate for dinner? I guess they have the same taste in both worlds."

A nervous chuckle escaped Christine as she nodded. "Maybe they have a universal menu for interdimensional travellers."

But their laughter was short-lived. As they continued to chat about their surroundings, a sudden chill filled the room. It was as though the walls themselves had ears, and every word they uttered was being heard by unseen forces.

In that eerie silence, they became aware that they might not be alone in this room. The sense of being watched, the feeling of an invisible presence, sent shivers down their spines.

Alex's eyes widened as he whispered, "Did you feel that? I think...someone was here, someone who heard every word we said."

Their hearts raced as they realized that they might not be the only ones with secrets in this enigmatic castle.

As they sat in the room, their minds racing with thoughts of the mysterious lion, Celine couldn't help but voice her suspicions. "Guys, remember the lion we encountered in the forest? What if it was Asena all along? Maybe she's been guiding us, testing us, and even sending the food."

Christine's eyes widened, and Alex nodded in contemplation. It was a theory that seemed increasingly plausible given the strange events they'd experienced.

Their conversation was abruptly cut short by the sound of a door closing in the distance. They exchanged nervous glances, their hearts pounding in their chests. It was as if the castle itself was listening and responding to their every word and action.

With the door now closed, they assumed that Asena had retired to her room for the night, perhaps to rest. Little did they know that the castle held secrets they had yet to uncover, and their journey was far from over. They understood that their time in the castle was growing shorter, and the final confrontation with Asena and the fate of the gem of life drew closer.

Inside their room, the three of them carefully crafted their plan as Asena's slumber continued. Celine, with determination in her eyes, took hold of the book that had been their guide throughout their perilous journey. Beside her, Alex gripped a knife, its blade gleaming dimly in the room's ambient light.

Christine watched with a mix of anticipation and trepidation.

In a synchronized motion, they made their move. Alex, with the knife at the ready, stepped forward and tested the doorknob to ensure no sound would betray them. Satisfied, he eased the door open, revealing the dimly lit corridor beyond.

Celine, her fingers gently grazing the book's cover, followed him as they ventured into the corridor, their steps barely making a sound. Their destination: Asena's room, the epicentre of the mysteries that had surrounded them.

The anticipation weighed heavy in the air as they silently and cautiously moved down the corridor. The weight of the book in Celine's hands and the glint of the knife in Alex's grip

CHAPTER 8

The Gem's Last Stand PART 1

Their quest for the gem of life led them through the labyrinthine corridors and hidden chambers of the castle. Each room they entered was a new puzzle, a challenge to their determination and resourcefulness.

The tension in the air thickened as minutes turned to hours, and the castle seemed to stretch into infinity. Shadows danced on the walls, and whispers of the past filled their ears, making their search feel like an eerie journey through time.

With each empty room and every hidden passage that led to a dead end, their hopes waned. The anticipation of finding the gem had driven them this far, but the weight of doubt pressed down on their shoulders.

As they moved from room to room, the unsettling feeling that they were not alone in the castle became more pronounced. A chill ran down their spines, and they exchanged nervous glances. It was as if the very walls were watching, and the history of the castle whispered dark secrets in their ears.

Christine's hand trembled as she pushed open a heavy wooden door, revealing a chamber filled with ancient tomes. Dust motes danced in the dim light, and the scent of aged paper filled the air.

"There must be something here," she whispered, her voice barely audible.

Alex, still holding the knife, nodded in agreement. "Keep searching. It's here somewhere."

Celine, her fingers tracing the intricate patterns on the book, felt a surge of determination. They had come too far to give up now. But with each empty room, the sense of urgency grew.

The castle held its secrets tightly, and they were determined to uncover the truth. They pressed on, driven by the hope that the gem of life was within their grasp, somewhere in the labyrinthine depths of Asena's domain.

Frustration and determination mingled as they stood at a crossroads in their search for the gem of life. Their footsteps echoed through the castle's vast halls as they shared a silent moment of agreement. It was time to divide and conquer.

"We can cover more ground this way," Alex suggested, his voice carrying a hint of urgency. "We'll find that gem, no matter what."

Christine nodded in agreement, her determination shining in her eyes. "Let's meet back here in an hour. If anyone finds anything, don't hesitate to shout."

With a collective nod, they parted ways, each venturing down a different corridor, their footsteps echoing into the distance. The castle's myriad secrets were about to be unveiled, one way or another.

As Celine roamed the halls, her fingers brushed against the cold, ancient stones. The air was thick with history, and she felt as if the very walls whispered forgotten tales. She checked each room with precision, her mind focused on the gem's elusive location.

In another wing of the castle, Alex's footsteps were steady as he moved through chambers filled with antique furnishings. His keen eyes scanned every nook and cranny, searching for any hidden compartments or concealed artifacts. The hope of finding the gem was a powerful motivator, and he pushed forward with unyielding determination.

Meanwhile, Christine explored the castle's library, her fingers trailing along the spines of countless books. She read titles, opened dusty tomes, and scoured the shelves for any hidden clues or information about the gem. The soft flickering of candlelight illuminated her path as she ventured deeper into the repository of knowledge.

The castle's mysteries seemed to expand with each passing minute, but the trio was undeterred. As they moved further away from one another, the urgency of their quest only grew, and the gem of life remained tantalizingly out of reach Celine's footsteps echoed through the dimly lit corridor as she ventured deeper into the heart of the castle. The air felt heavy with secrets, and a sense of foreboding settled over her. With each step, her heart pounded in her chest, and a shiver crawled down her spine.

She pushed open a heavy oak door, and what lay before her was a chilling sight. The room was bathed in an eerie red glow, and the walls were stained with dark, dried blood. A glass display case in the centre of the room held a majestic crown, encrusted with gleaming jewels, and a wooden staff adorned with intricate carvings.

The crown appeared both magnificent and sinister, its jewels reflecting the red light in a way that gave them an unsettling, almost malevolent glimmer. The staff, with its twisted, gnarled wood and haunting carvings, seemed like an artifact of dark magic.

Celine's breath caught in her throat as she approached the glass case. The room seemed to hum with an ominous energy, and she felt as if she had stumbled upon a forbidden chamber of dark rituals and ancient power. The blood-stained walls whispered stories of sacrifice and secrets too terrible to be told.

She couldn't tear her eyes away from the crown and staff, and an unshakable feeling of dread washed over her. There was a connection between these artifacts and the gem of life, but the nature of that connection remained elusive.

As she stood in that macabre room, Celine couldn't help but wonder about the history of the castle, the enigmatic Asena, and the true purpose of these sinister artifacts.

Christine wandered through the castle's labyrinthine corridors, drawn by the allure of the library. The chamber she entered was vast, and ancient tomes lined its shelves, their spines covered in dust and cobwebs. The air held a heavy scent of age and knowledge.

As she perused the titles, her fingers brushed against the leather-bound covers, sending shivers of excitement down her spine. The room was a treasure trove of arcane wisdom, and she marveled at the secrets held within those pages.

Her fascination was interrupted by a soft squelching sound beneath her shoes. Startled, she glanced down to find a wet carpet, and a sticky, dark substance clung to her shoe. Panic surged within her as she realized that it was fresh, and the source was nearby.

She strained her ears, and a muffled sound reached her. It was a low, guttural whisper, as if someone was speaking in hushed tones. Christine's heart raced as she looked around, trying to locate the source of the sound.

It seemed to emanate from a corner of the library, where a thick curtain concealed a hidden alcove. With trepidation, she approached, parting the curtain to reveal the alcove's contents. Her breath caught in her throat as she saw a huddled figure, cloaked in shadow, its face obscured.

Panic surged through Christine as she realized she was not alone in this chamber. In a rush of fear, she turned and fled from the library, the echoing footsteps of the unknown presence seemingly following her.

The library, once a sanctuary of knowledge, now felt like a dark and foreboding place. As Christine made her escape, she knew that there were mysteries within this castle that were far more menacing than any she had encountered before.

Alex's footsteps echoed through the quiet corridors of the castle as he searched for any sign of the gem of life or information that could lead them closer to their goal. The oppressive atmosphere of the castle weighed on him, and every creak of the floorboards felt like a whisper of secrets long buried.

His exploration led him to a room with a solitary computer on a dusty desk. The computer's screen flickered to life as if waiting for his arrival, revealing an opened browser with a webpage displaying detailed information about him, Celine, and Christine. Shock rippled through him as he read about their lives, their past, and their family histories. It was as if someone had been meticulously tracking their every move.

As he processed this unsettling revelation, the silence was shattered by the sound of shattering glass. It came from a nearby room, and his heart raced with a combination of fear and curiosity. He knew he had to investigate.

Alex left the computer behind and hurried into the adjacent room, his footsteps quick and determined. There, he found a broken glass jar on the floor, its contents spilled and scattered. The shattered jar had held an array of colourful, unidentifiable substances, and the smell in the air was strange and otherworldly.

Fear gnawed at him as he realized that someone—or something—had been in that room with him. He couldn't explain the strange occurrence, but it was clear that they were not alone in the castle, and that their every move was being watched.

Without hesitation, Alex turned and made his escape, his mind racing with questions and uncertainty. The castle held secrets far darker and more perilous than they had ever imagined, and it seemed that their every step was leading them deeper into a web of mystery and danger.

The three teens convened in the dimly lit hallway, their faces etched with anxiety and confusion. They had each stumbled upon unsettling discoveries within the castle, and it was evident that Asena's intentions were far more enigmatic and sinister than they had initially thought.

Celine, Christine, and Alex shared their findings with each other, their voices hushed in the eerie stillness of the castle. The revelations weighed heavily on their shoulders, and they exchanged concerned glances as they pieced together the fragments of the puzzle.

Just as they contemplated their next move, their attention was drawn to a nearby door—a door they had not previously explored. It was ajar, revealing a soft, inviting glow that spilled out into the hallway. The light was mesmerizing, beckoning them to investigate.

Approaching the door cautiously, they discovered it was Asena's room. The chamber was bathed in a soft, ethereal radiance, and an air of foreboding hung within. The room was immaculately tidy, every piece of furniture in its place, but it was the atmosphere that sent shivers down their spines.

In the center of the room lay the map, carefully laid out on the floor. Its intricate patterns and symbols were illuminated by the soft, magical glow. They realized that Asena was not merely a thief; she was a guardian of ancient knowledge and mystical power.

As they stood on the precipice of a revelation, a heavy silence enveloped them. The map held the key to understanding Asena's true purpose and the fate of the gem of life. With trepidation, they stepped into her room, each footfall echoing in the charged atmosphere.

Their journey had led them to this moment, where they would confront the enigmatic Asena and unlock the secrets of the gem. The room pulsed with anticipation, and the teenagers were acutely aware that the final, most perilous chapter of their quest was about to begin.

The anticipation in Asena's room hung thick in the air, and the map, with its cryptic symbols, was like a siren's call, drawing them further into the mystery. Celine, Christine, and Alex stood at the threshold of the room, ready to unveil the secrets concealed within.

However, just as they were about to step inside, Alex hesitated. He turned to the others with a lopsided grin. "You know what? I think I'll wait outside for this one. Guard the hallway, you know, in case of any unexpected visitors."

Celine couldn't help but chuckle. "Alex, you're not going to chicken out on us now, are you?"

Alex waved his hand dismissively. "No, no, not at all. I'm just, um, safeguarding our retreat, you know? Plus, I've seen enough strange things for one day. I'll be right out here, ready to sprint if need be."

Christine rolled her eyes but gave him an encouraging nod. "Alright, we'll hold down the fort. Don't wander too far, and don't get into any trouble out there."

With that, Celine and Christine entered Asena's room, leaving Alex standing guard in the hallway. He couldn't help but feel a mixture of relief and FOMO (Fear of Missing Out). As much as he wanted to stay clear of the eerie room, the thought of potentially missing out on crucial information gnawed at him.

He listened to their voices from outside, wondering what they would uncover and if this was the final piece of the puzzle they needed to understand the gem's true power and Asena's motives. It was a strange position to be in, waiting in the hallway while your friends ventured into the unknown, but Alex was determined to play his part, even if it was from a safe distance.

As Celine and Christine ventured further into Asena's room, their curiosity was piqued by the map, glowing softly on the floor. But their exploration was abruptly halted when their eyes fell on something else in the room—an innocuous-looking blanket draped across a chair.

As they approached, they exchanged puzzled glances. What could be hidden beneath it? With cautious anticipation, they pulled the blanket aside, revealing the form of Asena herself, curled up in a peaceful slumber.

They held their breath, fearing to disturb her rest, but their goal was the gem, and it lay just inches from Asena's grasp. Celine reached for it, her fingers brushing the cool, shimmering surface.

Just as they thought they had secured their prize, a bone-chilling presence filled the room, sending a shiver down their spines. They both turned to the source of the feeling and found Asena standing beside the door.

The sight was ghastly—Asena's eyes seemed to hold an otherworldly, malevolent gleam. She held a staff in her hand, a staff that pulsed with an eerie energy.

A smile curved on Asena's lips, but it was a smile devoid of warmth. "Hello, dear guests," she whispered in a tone that sent icy tendrils down their spines.

Celine's voice quivered as she uttered a single word, "Run."

The room transformed into a chilling battleground. Asena's staff crackled with power, and the gem of life, now a focal point of intense conflict, seemed to pulse with its own energy.

The teens scrambled for cover, seeking shelter from the magical onslaught that Asena had unleashed. The room became a maelstrom of light and darkness, as they grappled with their newfound adversary in a battle for the gem and their very lives.

As Celine, Christine, and Alex fled the room in terror, the oppressive presence of Asena's dark magic loomed over them. Their footsteps echoed through the castle's hallways as they sprinted for their lives. Panic gnawed at their hearts, and their breaths came in ragged gasps.

The grandeur of the castle's interior had become a claustrophobic maze, where every shadow seemed to conceal hidden threats. Their desperate flight led them through dimly lit corridors, their echoes amplifying their fear.

The fear of losing Celine propelled them forward, but she struggled to keep up, her footsteps faltering with exhaustion. Asena's malevolent laughter echoed ominously behind them, growing closer with each passing moment.

Celine's heart pounded in her chest, her breath a frantic rhythm in her ears. Her legs ached, and her vision blurred as terror took hold. She stumbled, nearly falling, and as her friends tried to help her, Asena seized the opportunity. With a surge of dark magic, she closed the distance between them in an instant, her presence sending a paralyzing chill through Celine's veins.

Asena's fingers wrapped around Celine's wrist, her grip like a vice. The room seemed to darken around them as Celine's struggles proved futile. Her eyes locked with Asena's, a chilling emptiness dwelling within the depths of the queen's gaze.

"You thought you could escape, my dear?" Asena's voice was a haunting whisper, like the sigh of a phantom. "Your determination is admirable, but your efforts are in vain. This gem of life is mine, and so are you."

Celine's pleas and cries were met with a sinister smile from Asena, who revelled in her despair. The room seemed to close in around them, the walls lined with ominous, shifting shadows.

In the dark heart of the castle, a battle of wills unfolded as Celine fought to resist Asena's dark influence. Her friends could only watch in horror as Celine's fate

hung in the balance, a dire reminder of the perilous path they had embarked upon.

As Christine and Celine emerged from the ominous castle, their faces were etched with fear and grief. The ordeal inside had shaken them to their core, and the weight of their friend's capture bore heavily on their hearts.

Outside, the forest loomed in all its eerie beauty, the trees shrouded in twilight. The rustling leaves seemed to whisper their foreboding secrets, and the distant hoot of an owl added to the night's chilling ambiance.

Christine's tears flowed freely as she clung to Alex, her sobs echoing through the dark woods. Her trembling voice carried the weight of her despair as she gasped for breath.

"It's all my fault," Christine choked out between sobs. "I should have been stronger, should have protected her."

Alex, his own eyes glistening with unshed tears, drew Christine into a comforting embrace. Her voice was a fragile whisper, resonating with both sorrow and a deep sense of unity.

"No, Christine," he said, his words tender and soothing. "We're in this together, and it's not your fault. We'll find a way to save her. We have to."

Alex stood by her side, his eyes filled with empathy and concern. He placed a reassuring hand on Christine's shoulder, offering his silent support.

As the friends clung to each other in the haunting depths of the forest, the challenges that lay ahead seemed insurmountable. The loss of their dear friend had left a void in their hearts, one that ached with the realization of the perils they had yet to face.

Inside the dimly lit chamber of Asena's castle, the atmosphere was heavy with tension and fear. Celine hung from a cold, unforgiving chain, her hands bound and her body bruised from the torment she had endured. Asena, the enigmatic villain who had manipulated their journey, stood before her, a sinister smile on her lips.

"Why did you help us, give us food, and then do this to me?" Celine rasped, her voice weak but filled with determination.

Asena's eyes bore into Celine's with a chilling intensity. "Oh, dear Celine," she hissed, "I helped you to get you here, to this castle, for you are the key to unlocking the gem's power. As a direct guardian of the gem, your presence is the final piece of the puzzle."

Celine's heart sank as the realization dawned upon her. She had unwittingly played a crucial role in Asena's dark plans. The room seemed to close in around them, the weight of their predicament pressing down on them like a suffocating shroud.

Asena's cruel laughter echoed through the chamber, and the fate of Celine, as well as the gem of life, hung in the balance, as they teetered on the brink of an uncertain future.

Asena, the malevolent sorceress, stood over Celine, her eyes filled with satisfaction as she prepared to cast a dark and binding spell. The incantation, ancient and powerful, was meant to bend the will of its victim, turning them into a loyal minion. Asena recited the words, her voice a cold, melodic chant, and her fingers weaved intricate patterns in the air.

In shadowed realm and twisted night, I

bind your will, I seize your sight. With

power dark and secrets held, Your

loyalty to me compelled.

Blood of guardian, now shall flow,

Bound to my will, as you shall know.

Celine, bound and helpless, was the unwilling subject of this dark sorcery. Asena's sinister intentions were to control her, to harness the unique power Celine possessed as a guardian of the gem.

Celine, struggling against her restraints, responded with a spell of her own. Her voice quivered, and her heart filled with defiance as she recited a counterincantation, her own words a whispered plea for liberation.

In the heart of courage, light does shine,

With strength of spirit, I now resign. As

shadows creep and bind my mind, I resist

the darkness, strength I find. With blood

of guardians, pure and true, I break these

chains, my will renewed.

Asena, unaware of Celine's efforts, continued to cast her spell, believing that her dark magic had succeeded in turning Celine into a loyal servant.

In this silent battle of spells, neither side was fully aware of the other's true intentions, setting the stage for a future confrontation that could tip the balance of power in this perilous game.

Asena, her cruel laughter echoing through the chamber, raised the gem high above her head. With a triumphant cry, she invoked the gem's power, causing its luminous green light to intensify. The room was bathed in an eerie, ethereal glow as the light grew stronger and stronger, casting sinister shadows on the walls.

The gem, pulsating with an otherworldly energy, seemed to respond to Asena's malevolence. Its verdant radiance filled the room, creating an atmosphere of foreboding. The very air hummed with power as the gem's magic surged, reinforcing her control over Celine and her dominance within the castle.

Asena's intentions were becoming clearer. The gem was the linchpin of her wicked plans, and the more it shone, the more her grasp over its dark abilities tightened.

In this pivotal moment, a formidable showdown was imminent. With Celine under her control and the gem's power at her command, Asena's malevolence had reached its peak. The destiny of all three teens and the fate of the world hung in the balance.

In the dense forest outside the castle, Alex and Christine huddled together, their faces etched with determination. Christine began to present a meticulously crafted plan, a strategy designed to outwit Asena and free Celine from her malevolent grasp.

"We need a foolproof plan," Christine asserted, her voice filled with resolve. "If we can approach Asena quietly, perhaps we can take her by surprise. With the right strategy, we can snatch the gem from her, break her control over Celine, and save the world."

Alex listened attentively, his brows furrowed in deep thought. He appreciated Christine's meticulous planning, but he knew that facing Asena required something entirely different. He shook his head, a determined glint in his eyes. "No, Christine," he countered, "a perfect plan won't work in this situation. Asena's magic is too powerful, and she's prepared for us. If we try to be too strategic, she'll sense it, and things will go south. We need to embrace the chaos, use it to our advantage. Let's create a diversion, stir up some trouble, and then make a dash for the gem."

Christine hesitated for a moment, considering Alex's unorthodox approach. In the end, she nodded, realizing the wisdom in his words. "You're right," she admitted. "In a situation like this, unpredictability might be our best weapon. Let's make our move."

With their plan set, Alex and Christine steeled themselves for the perilous journey back to the castle. The fate of Celine and the world depended on their ability to navigate the unpredictable path ahead.

As they ventured deeper into the forest, the canopy of ancient trees seemed to close in on them, creating an eerie darkness. They could hear the distant cawing of crows, their calls sounding like ominous warnings. The wind whispered through the leaves, carrying with it a sense of foreboding.

Alex and Christine knew they were approaching the castle, the heart of their challenge, and the potential epicentre of their peril. Their footsteps grew heavier, their breaths quickened, and their hearts beat like war drums in their chests.

The forest seemed to come alive around them, rustling leaves and crackling twigs hinting at unseen creatures. Shadows danced in the dim light, and every distant noise sent shivers down their spines. The world had become a place of uncertainty, a land where magic and danger intertwined.

Christine began to wonder about the countless challenges that lay ahead, each more treacherous than the last. As they moved forward, she couldn't help but recall the riddles, traps, and illusions they had faced earlier in their journey. Would they be prepared for what Asena had in store for them within the confines of her ominous castle?

As the duo pressed onward, their shared determination grew stronger. Alex's trust in the power of chaos and spontaneity gave them a unique sense of purpose, a belief that they could overcome even the darkest of obstacles. Christine couldn't help but admire his resilience and adaptability in the face of danger.

The forest before them seemed to stretch endlessly, the castle lurking in the distance like a foreboding shadow. The closer they came to it, the more they felt the weight of their mission. Alex and Christine knew they were ready for whatever lay ahead, for they possessed a weapon stronger than any magic or power – their unyielding determination to save their friend and the world.

With every step, they felt the castle drawing nearer, their resolve growing stronger. As they entered the castle's grounds, they knew that their greatest challenges and confrontations were yet to come.

Alex and Christine stood at the threshold of the imposing castle gate. The ancient stone structure loomed before them, an eerie silence enveloping its surroundings. The wind whispered through the cracks in the massive doors, like ghostly voices beckoning them to enter.

Alex's face betrayed his fear. His eyes darted from the foreboding gate to the darkened castle interior beyond. His heart pounded as a cold shiver crept down his spine. He turned to Christine, his voice trembling with trepidation. "I'm scared, Christine. This place... it's so sinister. What are we getting ourselves into?" Christine placed a comforting hand on his shoulder, her eyes filled with empathy and determination. "I know it's terrifying, Alex, but remember that we're not alone. Celine's life depends on us, and we're her only hope. We have to face our fears head-on, together."

Alex nodded, grateful for Christine's reassurance. He knew he couldn't let fear paralyze him. Celine was counting on them, and they couldn't afford to let her down.

With a deep breath, they steeled themselves for what lay ahead. The castle gate creaked ominously as they pushed it open, revealing a dark, cavernous hallway that stretched out before them. Their adventure had brought them this far, and they were determined to see it through to the end.

As they ventured further into the dimly lit corridor, the air grew colder, and the oppressive atmosphere weighed heavily on them. Shadows danced along the walls, and the eerie echoes of their footsteps were the only sounds that filled the void. It was as if the castle itself was holding its breath, waiting to unleash its secrets upon them.

Christine and Alex stayed close to each other, their footsteps echoing in unison. They shared an unspoken resolve – whatever lay ahead, they would face it together. The path they had chosen was treacherous and filled with danger, but they were prepared to navigate its twists and turns.

With each step they took deeper into the castle, they felt an unsettling sense of anticipation. Their every sense was heightened, as they knew that every corner could hide a new challenge, a fresh obstacle. But they pressed on, hearts filled with hope, knowing that they had come too far to turn back now.

As they ventured further into the shadows of the castle, their faith in each other and their cause grew stronger. They had faced countless trials, and now they stood on the precipice of their ultimate test. The fate of their friend, and perhaps the entire world, rested on their shoulders.

The dimly lit hallway stretched before them, its secrets and dangers hidden in the darkness. Alex and Christine knew that their journey was far from over, and with every step they took, they drew closer to the heart of their destiny.

TO BE CONTINUED IN THE NEXT CHAPTER

CHAPTER 9

The Gem's Last Stand PART 2

Outside the castle, Alex and Christine huddled in the dense forest. Fear loomed large, but they knew that their friend, Celine, was in grave danger, and they had to do everything in their power to rescue her.

Christine began outlining a plan, her voice filled with determination, "We have to sneak back into the castle quietly. We need to locate Celine and figure out a way to break her free without alerting Asena."

However, Alex, looking pale and anxious, interrupted, "No, Christine. We can't follow a meticulously planned rescue operation here. Asena's magic is too unpredictable, and if she senses our plan, it could lead to catastrophe. We must take a risk."

Christine blinked in surprise, her eyes filled with worry. "A risk? What do you mean, Alex?"

With a resolute look, Alex explained, "We have to go with the flow, Christine. Asena won't be expecting us to return to the castle so soon, especially not after we fled. We can use this element of surprise to our advantage. We need to approach this situation with an open mind and adapt to whatever comes our way. Let's make haste and reach the castle as soon as we can. When we're inside, we'll assess the situation and act accordingly."

Christine, although taken aback by this unconventional approach, understood the logic behind it. She nodded and said, "You're right, Alex. Let's go with the flow and be prepared for the unexpected. We're in this together, and we'll bring Celine back safely."

With newfound determination, they readied themselves to return to the foreboding castle, understanding that the unknown path that lay ahead would be fraught with challenges and surprises.

Celine, who had been enduring Asena's presence and her cruel tricks, spotted her friends, Alex and Christine, as they stealthily entered the room. Her eyes lit up with a subtle glint of relief as she tried to convey a secret message without alerting Asena.

Celine played her part, allowing Asena to believe she was under her control. "Asena," she said with a wicked grin, "How clever you are, creating these games. It's almost like you're showing off."

Asena, who had always been self-assured, couldn't help but bask in the praise. "You see, Celine, intelligence is a gift. Those who possess it must flaunt it for the world to see."

But beneath her facade of control, Celine's mind raced with a plan, a plan she hoped Alex and Christine would understand without any words. She knew that any indication of defiance would result in harsh consequences.

As Alex and Christine entered the room, they maintained their pretence, making it appear as if they were submitting to Asena's authority. Inwardly, however, they understood the unspoken message in Celine's wink and her words: *Play along, but be ready for the right moment.*

The game of wits had just begun, and the trio was determined to outsmart Asena to reclaim the gem and their freedom.

As Alex and Christine made their entrance into the room, they maintained their act of submission to Asena. Christine couldn't help herself and playfully greeted Asena with an enthusiastic, "Assie, hiya!"

Asena's eyes widened in disbelief as she muttered, "How the hell...?"

Alex joined in the charade, giving her a casual wave. "Hey, Assie, long time no see!"

A perplexed Asena struggled to comprehend the sudden shift in her prisoners' behaviour. She had expected resistance and defiance, not this unexpected familiarity.

The subtle mind games were taking a toll on Asena, leaving her rattled. Celine's clever tactics were already sowing the seeds of doubt and confusion. It was a strategic move to disarm their captor, setting the stage for their daring escape.

As the tension reached its peak in the room, Alex decided to make a daring move. He grabbed a hefty stone and hurled it directly at Asena. However, she was quick to react, wielding her formidable magic to deflect the projectile. Instead of striking her, the stone was redirected with force, sending Alex hurtling through the air and crashing into an unknown location.

Meanwhile, Asena was becoming increasingly agitated. She unleashed a barrage of spells, hurling them toward Celine and Christine, who were barely managing to dodge and evade. The room was filled with the crackling energy of their confrontation, making it a truly intense and perilous scene.

Amidst the chaos, Celine stumbled and fell to the ground. In her fall, the bag containing the book was flung open. She glanced at the book, which fell open to a section titled "The Guardians." Her heart raced as she read the ominous passage that described how the guardians could unlock incredible powers by making physical contact with the gem.

This revelation sent shivers down her spine. It was a terrifying realization that held the key to their survival, but it also meant confronting the formidable Asena.

With the knowledge of the guardians' power fresh in her mind, Celine quickly whispered the information to Christine as they ran from Asena's magical onslaught. Their hearts pounded as they realized their fate depended on embracing the incredible potential contained within the gem.

In the heat of the moment, they reached out and made physical contact with the gleaming gem, each of them pressing a hand upon its radiant surface. The second their fingers brushed against it, an electrifying sensation surged through their bodies. Their clothes shimmered and transformed, materializing into magnificent, sparkling frocks that matched their newfound, extraordinary abilities.

Christine and Celine felt a rush of power like never before, and suddenly, they began to float in mid-air. Asena's eyes widened with astonishment as she watched the sisters rise above her, their majestic gowns trailing behind them.

As Asena's powers clashed with those of Celine and Christine, the battleground became a chaotic frenzy of fire bolts and magical spells. The air crackled with energy, and the three of them engaged in a fierce magical duel.

The sisters, now wearing dazzling frocks from their newfound powers, fought bravely, launching fire bolts at Asena while trying to dodge her counterattacks. The forest around them lit up with bursts of magical flames, and the clash between good and evil was intense.

But Asena, being a formidable opponent, had tricks up her sleeve. With a wave of her staff, she summoned a cage made of ethereal energy, trapping both Celine and Christine inside. The two sisters were helpless, their magical powers rendered useless in the mystical prison.

Asena grinned wickedly, believing she had finally secured victory. The magical cage was impenetrable, and the gem was within her reach. But she underestimated the strength of the bond between the two sisters and the power that emanated from their connection. The gem pulsed with newfound energy, and the frocks they wore glowed even brighter.

With determination in their eyes, Celine and Christine joined their powers and pressed their hands against the gem. The cage quivered, and the magical energy within it began to wane. They focused all their energy on breaking free, and the cage cracked under the combined force of their wills.

As Asena revelled in her temporary victory and laughed menacingly, a sudden rumbling in the ground caught her attention. She looked around in bewilderment as the forest seemed to come to life.

The creatures of the forest, the very same beings the trio had encountered and won over during their journey, rushed to the scene. Massive bears, swift wolves, graceful deer, and a myriad of birds descended upon the area. They were united in their determination to help the sisters and free them from Asena's clutches.

With a deafening roar, the bear and the wolves began to claw and gnash at the magical cage. The birds cawed and fluttered, pecking at the mystical barriers. Their combined efforts sent tremors through the ground as they relentlessly worked to break the enchantment.

Asena's laughter turned to frustration, and she attempted to cast more spells to keep the animals at bay. But the united force of nature was too powerful. With a final, resounding burst of strength, the animals shattered the cage into thousands of sparkling fragments. Celine and Christine fell to the ground, gasping for breath but free at last.

Asena, realizing she was outnumbered the animals had come to their rescue, and their bond with nature had proven to be their greatest ally. It was a triumphant moment for the sisters, knowing that the forest had recognized them as its true guardians. They owed their victory to the friends they had made along the way and the powers bestowed upon them by the gem.

The battle raged on in the heart of the forest, with Asena standing at its centre, her staff radiating dark energy. She unleashed a relentless torrent of shadowy creatures that moved to engage the guardians and their newfound animal allies.

The gem's power coursed through Celine and Christine, and they felt a deep connection with the forest's creatures, which were now prepared to fight alongside them. Wolves, bears, birds, and an array of other animals gathered to support the sisters.

Asena summoned a storm of dark forces, sending them forth like a tempest. Swirling tendrils of darkness extended toward the guardians, but the animals, unified in their loyalty, rushed forward to confront the malevolent menace. The forest roared with the tumult of the battle, a chaotic symphony of bravery and determination.

Celine, her heart filled with newfound courage, raised her hand, and a burst of fire erupted, scorching the shadowy creatures with each strike. Christine, with her book of spells, chanted incantations that formed protective barriers for the forest's creatures, safeguarding them from the darkness.

Asena was a formidable adversary, her staff crackling with dark energy as she released spells with malicious intent. Lightning bolts, shadows, and fierce winds swirled around her. With a determined grimace, she unleashed her dark magic at Celine and Christine. The guardians countered with their newfound abilities, creating an explosive clash of vibrant energy and shadowy magic.

The forest animals displayed remarkable courage, each species contributing to the battle in its own unique way. Wolves leaped fearlessly at shadowy foes, tearing them apart with unmatched ferocity, while bears used their mighty paws to swat the spectral entities into oblivion. Birds dived from the treetops, striking the dark creatures with uncanny precision.

Asena's minions, once numerous and menacing, gradually began to falter. The combined might of the guardians and their animal allies was proving to be too much for the shadowy horde. Realizing that the battle had turned against her, Asena launched a final surge of dark power, targeting Celine and Christine directly.

In a desperate attempt to protect her sister, Christine invoked a spell from her book. An incantation created a radiant shield that enveloped them, forming a sanctuary against Asena's dark assault. The sphere of light pushed back the malevolent magic, sending shockwaves rippling outward that eradicated the lingering shadows.

As the last remnants of Asena's minions were obliterated by the collective efforts of the guardians and their animal allies, the dark queen herself continued to wield her staff, determined to overcome the sisters.

Exhausted yet triumphant, Celine, Christine, and the forest's creatures celebrated their hard-fought victory. Their connection with nature and the gem's power had not only vanquished Asena's dark forces but also solidified their role as protectors of the forest. With the gem in their possession, they were prepared to face any challenges that lay ahead.

With the battle against Asena won, the forest should have been filled with joy and relief. But suddenly, Asena unleashed a spell of unprecedented power. Her staff radiated with dark energy as she chanted incantations that shook the very foundations of the forest. A massive, shimmering wall of magic emerged, encircling the entire castle. The forest's creatures, who had fought bravely by the guardians' side, were now trapped outside the bewitched barrier.

Celine, Christine, and the animals watched in horror as the shimmering wall solidified, creating an impenetrable barrier that separated them from the castle and Asena. The sisters desperately reached out with their newfound powers, but the magic was beyond their control.

With the incantation complete, Asena's final act of desperation had dire consequences. Two of her remaining minions, twisted creatures who were once creatures of the forest, emerged from the castle, wielding their own dark powers. With a malevolent glint in their eyes, they flanked Asena, ready to do her bidding.

But Asena was not finished. She turned her attention to the animals beyond the barrier, focusing her dark powers with cruel intent. With a wave of her staff, she sent bolts of shadowy energy raining down upon the forest creatures. It was a relentless, devastating onslaught that left no chance for defence or escape.

Wolves, bears, birds, and an array of other animals that had fought valiantly alongside the guardians now perished in a storm of darkness. The forest was filled with mournful cries, and the guardians' hearts ached as they watched their newfound allies vanish one by one. The once jubilant forest was now a place of sorrow and loss.

Tears welled up in Celine's and Christine's eyes as they witnessed the destruction of their newfound friends. The sisters' grief was overwhelming, for they had developed a deep bond with these creatures in such a short time. The survivors watched with heavy hearts as one animal after another succumbed to Asena's merciless magic.

Amid the chaos, one creature remained untouched by Asena's onslaught: a majestic horse that stood apart from the rest. It gazed at the guardians with eyes that held a silent understanding as if sharing their grief and determination to confront the dark queen.

Asena's cackle of triumph echoed within the castle walls. She had used her minions and her dark powers to claim victory, decimating the forest's creatures who had dared to defy her. With her malevolent laughter lingering in the air, she readied herself for the final confrontation with the guardians.

Celine, Christine, and the surviving animals, their spirits heavy with grief and determination, now faced a grim reality. Asena was growing more powerful and more ruthless by the moment, and the ultimate battle between good and evil was about to reach its fateful climax.

Asena, her face twisted in a sinister grin, raised her staff high above her head, ready to cast a malevolent spell that could tip the scales of the confrontation. The room crackled with dark energy as she chanted the incantation, her eyes ablaze with wicked intent. The guardians braced themselves for the impending onslaught.

But before she could release her dark magic, something inexplicable occurred. The staff in her hand began to tremble violently, and dark energies swirled chaotically around her. Asena's triumphant expression quickly faded, replaced by one of confusion and dread. The incantation, intended to obliterate the guardians, spiralled out of control, forming a vortex of raw power that spun around her. With a cry of terror, she was engulfed by her own spell.

Asena was thrown backward, her body tumbling across the chamber as she screamed in fear and agony. Her staff, once a source of her dark strength, clattered to the ground, its power now uncontrollable. The guardians watched in astonishment as she crashed into a wall, disoriented and gasping for breath.

And then, Alex emerged from the shadows. His eyes glittered with determination as he stepped forward, holding another staff in his hands – the staff Asena had used earlier to transform her clothing into a dazzling frock. But what was truly remarkable was the gem he now held in his other hand, the same gem that had been the object of their perilous journey.

With a triumphant grin, Alex explained the audacious plan he had hatched when he noticed Asena's wardrobe change. Realizing that her garments contained the essence of her powers, he had taken the opportunity to swap staffs when Asena was distracted. The staff he had chosen was a mere replica, devoid of the dark enchantments that had allowed Asena to command her minions and wield her destructive magic.

Celine and Christine watched in awe as their companion, Alex, outwitted the formidable sorceress. The guardians had conspired to deceive their cunning adversary, using her own arrogance and vanity against her. With each passing moment, Asena's grip on her dark powers began to wane.

Celine, her eyes glittering with mischief, had played a pivotal role in the ruse. Pretending to be Asena's loyal minion, she had whispered false incantations to the sorceress, convincing her that her words of power were working as intended. The deception was so convincing that Asena, consumed by her overconfidence, had failed to notice the treachery.

As a result, the spell that should have unleashed destruction upon the guardians had been deliberately sabotaged. Asena's loss of control over her own magic, combined with Alex's quick thinking, had tipped the balance of power in Favor of the guardians.

Asena, weakened and disoriented, tried to rise but found herself unable to muster the strength. The gem she sought to control was now in the guardians' hands. The tables had turned, and she was now at their mercy.

The guardians exchanged triumphant glances, having succeeded in outsmarting their formidable adversary. The decisive moment had come, and Asena was now vulnerable, her reign of darkness hanging in the balance. It was a testament to their wit and courage, marking a pivotal turning point in their quest to stop Asena's malevolent ambitions.

Alex, now transformed into a coat, discovered the magical potential of the gem as he desperately tried to harness its power. His coat form shimmered with a mystical light, and he could feel the energy coursing through him. The gem had granted him the means to resist Asena's attempts at subjugation.

Asena, still reeling from the chaos she had inadvertently unleashed upon herself, attempted one last, desperate gambit to sway the guardians to her side. Gasping and disoriented, she extended a trembling hand toward them, her voice laced with desperation.

"Join me," she implored. "With your power and mine, we can reshape this world. You can share in my dominion."

Celine and Christine exchanged resolute glances. They were tempted by the lure of power but remembered the values they had upheld throughout their perilous journey. They shook their heads in unison, steadfast in their resolve.

"We've come too far to be swayed by the darkness," Celine declared.

With those words, a powerful current of water, summoned by the guardians' unity, surged around Asena. It formed an impenetrable barrier, a watery cage, trapping her within its swirling, liquid walls. Asena's cries of outrage were silenced as the magical prison held her fast.

The guardians had managed to subdue the malevolent sorceress, using the gem's newfound magic to their advantage. With Asena trapped and her powers contained, her reign of darkness was finally at an end. The threat she had posed to the world could no longer harm the innocent.

Now, the guardians were left with a decision – to safeguard the gem and prevent it from falling into the wrong hands or to destroy it entirely to eliminate its potential for chaos. Their journey had been fraught with challenges and had tested their courage, wisdom, and unity. As they stood before the watery cage that contained their adversary, they knew that their final decision would determine the fate of the gem and the world itself.

As the watery cage surrounding Asena dissolved, the castle began to change. The once-darkened fortress was no longer encased in a mystical barrier. The haunting green light faded away, but there was no miraculous resurrection of the fallen animals. The world outside remained untouched by the chaotic magic that had enveloped the castle.

Celine, Christine, and Alex looked at one another, their faces reflecting the sadness that had accompanied their journey. The sacrifices and losses they had endured could not be undone. However, they knew that they had accomplished much on their journey. The gem was now safe, Asena was defeated, and they had grown as individuals and as friends.

With a heavy heart, they opened the book once more, hoping to find guidance on their next steps. The pages revealed a riddle that would lead them to the next challenge. The guardians were to seek out the ancient oak tree, a place imbued with wisdom and secrets. But to reach it, they would have to solve a challenge that remained unknown, a test of their resolve, wits, and unity.

The three friends knew that their journey was far from over. They had faced adversity and danger together, and they were determined to overcome the challenges that lay ahead. With a shared sense of purpose and the gem safely in their possession, they embarked on the path to find the ancient oak tree, where answers and further trials awaited them.

Celine opened the mystical book, and its pages revealed a riddle, written in shimmering letters of emerald green. As she read it aloud to her companions, the words echoed through the forest:

"In shadows deep, your fears will rise,   Confront

them now, don't close your eyes. Each guardian,

you must face your dread, In unity, your strength

shall spread.

A past's mistakes, a future's unknown,

The specters of your fears have grown.

Within this wood, your doubts you'll meet,

But with friendship strong, they'll see defeat.

At the ancient oak, your path's unfold,

Embrace your strength, let courage hold.

Face your fears, accept your might,

For in unity, you'll find the light."

The riddle's words resonated with the guardians, and they knew they had to embark on this challenge to reach the ancient oak tree and continue their quest.

Determined by the riddle, the three guardians ventured deeper into the forest, where the looming trees cast elongated shadows. As they moved forward, their breaths quickened, and the tension in the air grew heavier. Celine, Christine, and Alex could feel a growing sense of apprehension, knowing that the challenge ahead would test them to their limits.

After a long trek, they arrived at a clearing encircled by gnarled, ancient oaks, their branches swaying like ghostly fingers in the night. In the centre of the clearing stood an ominous, shadowy figure, shrouded in a mist that seemed to emanate from the very ground itself.

The figure coalesced into their deepest fears, taking shape as monstrous creatures, nightmares from their pasts, and otherworldly beings. Celine faced a nightmarish version of herself, representing the guilt she felt for her childhood choices. Christine encountered a spectral librarian who embodied the fear of failure and lost knowledge. Alex was confronted by a digital abyss, his darkest fear of technological isolation and loneliness.

Each guardian knew that they had to confront and conquer their deepest fears. The ethereal entities taunted and tormented them, using their greatest insecurities against them. As they fought these nightmarish manifestations, the forest around them transformed, becoming an eerie dreamscape where reality and illusion blurred.

Celine summoned her inner strength, facing her nightmarish self. She accepted her past mistakes and forgave herself, banishing her doppelganger. Her courage and self-acceptance dispersed the dark spectre.

Christine, determined not to let her fear of failure control her, stood her ground.

She challenged the spectral librarian with her own knowledge and wit, finally proving that she was not defined by her past mistakes or the pressure of expectations.

Alex realized that he had been running from his fear of isolation instead of embracing it. He engaged in a heated debate with the digital abyss, questioning the value of constant connection. In the end, he realized that technology should enhance, not replace, genuine human connection.

With each guardian conquering their deepest fears, the nightmares began to dissipate, and the eerie dreamscape reverted to a tranquil clearing. The ominous figure that had summoned their fears slowly dissipated, leaving the ancient oaks bathed in the silvery light of the moon.

The guardians gathered in the middle of the clearing, shaken but victorious. They had demonstrated their courage, unity, and strength by facing their most profound fears and doubts. As they continued on their quest, the path ahead became clearer, leading them to the ancient oak tree and the final stages of their extraordinary journey.

Leaving the clearing, the guardians felt renewed and emboldened. The challenge in the shadowy grove had strengthened their resolve, bringing them even closer together. As they ventured deeper into the forest, they began to notice subtle changes in the environment. The air grew cooler, and the ancient trees around them seemed to whisper secrets from ages past.

They followed the instructions from the enchanted book, making their way through the woods with determination. The surroundings became more mysterious, with bioluminescent mushrooms casting an eerie glow along the path, and the faint sound of a distant river flowing.

After hours of wandering through the mystical forest, the guardians reached a peculiar area where the trees had peculiar, twisted trunks. The grove was illuminated by the soft, ethereal light of fireflies that danced through the night.

The book suddenly began to shimmer, its pages flipping open on their own. A new riddle emerged, glowing with a faint green light:

"In a forest of mystic might,

Where the ancient trees take flight,

The path ahead is veiled in woe,

With tricks and puzzles that ebb and flow.

To find the way and face the test,

Unlock your minds and be your best.

Navigate this labyrinth's spell,

Where illusions dance and secrets dwell."

As the riddle faded, the path ahead twisted and turned, revealing a complex, shifting labyrinth of illusions. The guardians were surrounded by an otherworldly maze of shimmering walls that appeared and disappeared as if made of mist. Eerie whispers echoed through the labyrinth, tempting and misleading them.

The guardians shared a look, understanding that they were about to embark on a challenge that would push their wits and teamwork to the limit. With the wisdom they had gained in the shadowy grove, they entered the Labyrinth of Illusions, prepared to confront whatever enigmatic trials lay ahead.

As they delved further into the labyrinth, their surroundings shifted with every step, and they could never be sure whether the path they saw was real or just another illusion. Challenges and conundrums awaited them around every corner, and the path was fraught with optical tricks and shifting walls that played with their perceptions.

The guardians pushed forward, navigating the surreal labyrinth with careful thought and communication. Some illusions tried to lead them astray, but the lessons they had learned from conquering their deepest fears served them well. With unity, resolve, and clever problem-solving, they continued to inch closer to the centre of the Labyrinth of Illusions, where the valuable artifact or piece of information they sought awaited them.

As they progressed deeper into the maze, they also grew closer as friends and allies. The journey had tested their limits and brought them face to face with their most profound fears, but it had also revealed their strength and the unbreakable bond that held them together. The guardians knew that they could face any challenge, no matter how surreal, as long as they faced it together.

The Labyrinth of Illusions would prove to be an unforgettable chapter in their remarkable adventure, and as they overcame each challenge, they moved one step closer to their ultimate goal.

As the guardians ventured deeper into the Labyrinth of Illusions, they encountered a range of puzzling challenges that tested their problem-solving skills and their ability to distinguish reality from illusion. One of the first challenges they faced was an illusionary barrier that seemed to block their path. The barrier shifted and shimmered, making it nearly impossible to discern where it began and ended.

Alex, being the tech-savvy member of the group, pulled out his phone and started capturing videos and images of the barrier from different angles. He reasoned that by studying the images, they might discover patterns or clues that would help them navigate through it. The rest of the group watched as he worked, providing suggestions and encouragement along the way.

Their combined efforts eventually revealed a subtle pattern in the shifting barrier's movements. By carefully timing their movements and exploiting the patterns they had discovered, they managed to slip through the illusionary barrier unscathed.

Their journey through the Labyrinth of Illusions continued, leading them into an area filled with hallucinatory echoes of distant voices. The guardians struggled to concentrate as the voices whispered, shouted, and conversed. It was as if the maze itself was trying to disorient them, making it difficult to discern their true surroundings from the illusion.

Christine felt the confusion setting in and raised her voice to speak over the spectral voices, trying to rally her companions. "Don't listen to the whispers! Keep your minds focused on each other and our goal!"

Her words served as an anchor, pulling the group together as they pressed forward, determined to overcome the auditory illusions. Despite the overwhelming distractions, their shared resolve and unity allowed them to push through the disorienting voices.

Eventually, they encountered a large wall that seemed to block their path. Carved into the stone was a complex script of symbols and equations, a seemingly insurmountable challenge. The guardians quickly understood that they had to decode the wall to proceed, but they had only three chances to do so.

Alex began to examine the strange script, recognizing the intricate patterns of mathematical symbols that hinted at an elaborate puzzle. With the first attempt, he started translating the symbols and equations into a comprehensible message.

Celine and Christine watched with bated breath as Alex worked, his face reflecting a mixture of concentration and determination. But his first two attempts led to a sense of disappointment as they proved incorrect, extinguishing two of their precious chances.

As despair threatened to creep in, Alex's memory triggered a recollection of a complex algorithm he had learned in his computer science studies. The algorithm provided a solution that felt both perplexing and ingenious, and it was different from his initial approach.

With renewed hope, he began typing out the complex algorithm with practiced precision. The script on the wall shifted and transformed as he worked, revealing the intricate dance of numbers and symbols he was crafting.

Their hearts raced as he entered the final lines of code, and the wall responded, its surface reconfiguring into a clear passage forward. The guardians celebrated their victory with relieved smiles, knowing that Alex's ingenious algorithm had led them through the cryptic script.

"Alex, you're a genius!" Christine exclaimed, her admiration for his problemsolving skills evident in her eyes.

Celine added, "That was incredible, Alex. I knew you'd figure it out."

With a grin, Alex shared his triumphant moment with his companions. "I just remembered a little something from my studies. Sometimes, you need to think outside the box."

However, the true test was yet to come, and the guardians pressed forward into the heart of the labyrinth.

As they journeyed deeper into the maze of illusions, the guardians came across increasingly bizarre and complex challenges. Their unity and resourcefulness would continue to be their greatest assets as they sought to unlock the secrets of the Labyrinth of Illusions.

As they proceeded deeper into the Labyrinth of Illusions, their challenges grew more intricate and their resolve stronger. They faced illusions that tested their sense of reality and their ability to discern truth from deception.

One of the most perplexing challenges they encountered was a series of seemingly endless mirrors that stretched in all directions. The reflections within these mirrors played tricks on their minds, showing them alternative paths and confusing their sense of direction. It was as if the very essence of the maze was toying with their perception of reality.

In the midst of this mirrored maze, Alex couldn't help but crack a joke, attempting to lighten the mood. "Who knew we'd end up in a labyrinth of hallways with mirrors? Looks like we're trapped in a funhouse."

Christine chuckled, appreciating his humour. "Well, at least we know we're the guardians of laughter, too."

Celine smiled, agreeing, "Laughter is indeed a powerful tool, especially in the face of illusions."

While their jests brought a brief moment of levity, they understood that they needed to find a way out of the mirrored maze. They couldn't rely on humour alone, so they focused on their unique abilities.

Christine's connection to nature led her to seek guidance from the flora around them. She asked the plants for help in navigating through the maze, and they responded by revealing hidden pathways and guiding them toward the correct route. With the assistance of the living labyrinth, they began to discern the illusion from reality and made their way forward.

Their progress was marked by increasing awareness of the intricate interplay between illusion and reality, and it became evident that the Labyrinth of Illusions was a place where their strengths as guardians would be continually challenged. Each step they took required not only their intelligence but also their unity and their unwavering determination to protect the gem.

The next challenge led them to a room filled with countless floating orbs, each emitting a faint, mesmerizing glow. These orbs cast ethereal shadows on the walls, creating a hypnotic display that threatened to draw them into a trance.

As they stood at the threshold of this enigmatic room, they exchanged knowing glances. They understood that the orbs held their deepest fears and anxieties, luring them to confront the aspects of themselves they had long buried.

Christine took a step forward, her voice steady but filled with determination. "We must face our fears together. These orbs are testing us, but they cannot break our unity."

Celine and Alex nodded in agreement. They each reached out to touch one of the floating orbs, prepared to confront the illusions that lay within. The moment their hands made contact with the orbs, their fears materialized before them in vivid, surreal displays.

For Alex, it was a haunting vision of his mother, who had left him when he was just a four-month-old baby. She appeared before him, her eyes filled with disappointment and sadness. His chest tightened as he relived the abandonment he had always carried as a heavy burden.

Celine confronted her deepest fear as well, a vision of being isolated from her friends and loved ones, unable to protect them when they needed her most. She felt the crushing weight of isolation and powerlessness, and it threatened to consume her.

Christine's fear manifested as the image of a dying forest, where she could hear the cries of wounded animals. She watched helplessly as the environment she cherished deteriorated, her heart breaking with each tree that fell and each animal that perished.

Yet, in the face of their deepest fears, the guardians drew strength from each other. They called out to one another and shared their fears openly. As they did, the illusions lost their grip. Alex, Celine, and Christine realized that they were stronger together, their unity a powerful force that shattered the illusions one by one.

With their fears dispelled, the orbs lost their allure. The room's ethereal glow faded, and they continued on their journey, more determined than ever to overcome whatever challenges the Labyrinth of Illusions had in store for them.

The guardians recognized that the road ahead would be fraught with illusions and deceptions, but they remained unyielding in their resolve to protect the gem and fulfil their mission.

The guardians continued to navigate the perplexing labyrinth, each challenge forging a deeper connection among them. As they progressed, they encountered another formidable test.

In a room filled with towering crystal pillars, the guardians were met with a dazzling display of their own reflections. The mirrored walls created a maze of endless corridors, and their own images were multiplied countless times, stretching into infinity. It was as if they stood at the heart of a kaleidoscope, and their reflections danced around them, mirroring their every move.

Celine's voice was laced with amusement as she quipped, "Looks like we're starring in our own cosmic dance show."

Christine joined in the light-heartedness, adding, "I guess this is the guardians' version of a grand ball."

Alex, ever the pragmatist, couldn't resist a smile. "If this is a ball, I hope we remember the steps."

But their humour soon faded as they realized the true nature of the challenge. The reflection maze was meant to disorient them, to challenge their ability to distinguish reality from illusion. The crystal pillars, which held a powerful enchantment, played tricks on their senses, compelling them to follow deceptive pathways.

Their determination to reach the Oak Tree propelled them forward. They needed to pass this illusionary dance and claim the gem. As they ventured deeper into the maze of reflections, the guardians noticed that the mirrors were not only creating deceptive paths but also obscuring concealed symbols on the floor, depicting the correct route.

Amidst the labyrinth of mirrored images, Celine suddenly stopped. "Wait, I've got it. Those symbols on the floor are the key. They show us the way."

Christine and Alex nodded in agreement. Following the symbols etched on the floor, they began to navigate the labyrinth with a newfound sense of direction. The reflections, though numerous, could not obscure the truth of the symbols. Step by step, they advanced along the path.

The guardians encountered moments of uncertainty as the reflections attempted to distract and disorient them. Yet, the unity of the guardians and their shared understanding of the labyrinth's deceptions became their strength.

Finally, they reached the centre of the crystal maze. Before them stood the Oak Tree, its ancient branches stretching toward the ceiling. Its roots were intricately intertwined with the crystal pillars, symbolizing the guardians' connection to the world and their resolve to protect it.

Celine couldn't help but marvel at the sight. "This is it, the Oak Tree. It's magnificent."

Christine gazed at the tree with a sense of reverence. "Our journey has led us here. Let's fulfil our purpose and protect the gem."

Alex, his gaze unwavering, said, "Together, we'll ensure that Asena's power is no longer a threat to the world."

As they prepared to reach for the gem, the room surrounding them seemed to ripple with energy, as if the Oak Tree itself acknowledged their presence. The moment was charged with anticipation as they reached out to fulfil their destiny and claim the gem that held the key to the world's protection.

With the gem in hand, the guardians knew that the final chapter of their mission was near, and the challenges that lay ahead would be the ultimate test of their strength and unity. They were ready to face whatever awaited them with unwavering determination and the boundless power of the gem at their side.

As the guardians reverently placed the gem at the base of the ancient Oak Tree, the world around them seemed to shift and shimmer. The ground rumbled beneath their feet, and the air pulsed with a newfound energy. The guardian gem, now reunited with its rightful place, emitted a radiant green light that surged through the tree's gnarled branches and roots, infusing every part of it.

The Oak Tree responded to the gem's return by shedding its age-old bark, revealing a vibrant and luminescent trunk beneath. Its leaves rustled with a renewed vitality, and the forest around them came alive in a symphony of colors, sounds, and life. Birds perched on the branches, their songs harmonizing with the rustling leaves. The sun broke through the canopy, casting a warm and comforting glow over the rejuvenated forest.

The entire world seemed to breathe a sigh of relief, echoing the guardians' own feelings of triumph. Their mission was a success; the gem's power had been restored, and the world was healing. It was as if nature itself had awakened from a long slumber, ready to flourish once more.

Celine, Christine, and Alex gazed in awe at the transformed Oak Tree, their hearts filled with a profound sense of accomplishment. The gem's energy pulsed within them, a constant reminder of their duty as protectors of the world.

With a smile, Christine said, "We did it. The world is safe once again."

Alex nodded, his expression reflecting a mixture of relief and pride. "And we did it together, as the guardians we were destined to be."

Celine, her voice filled with gratitude, added, "And we have each other, the power of the gem, and the strength to face whatever challenges may lie ahead."

As they continued to stand beneath the now-resplendent Oak Tree, they knew that their journey was far from over. More adventures and challenges awaited them, but they were ready. With the gem's power and their unbreakable bond, there was no obstacle they couldn't overcome.

The guardians had fulfilled their destiny, and the world, bathed in the light of the Oak Tree and the guardian gem, held the promise of a brighter, more harmonious future. Together, they would face whatever challenges arose, united by their unwavering dedication to protecting the world they loved.

As the guardians made their way back to the castle, they noticed that Asena was nowhere to be found. Her absence raised questions, and a sense of uncertainty lingered in the air. Yet, the guardians shared a collective determination. They knew that their journey had transformed them, making them stronger, wiser, and more united than ever before.

With resolute expressions, they looked at one another and nodded. Whatever awaited them, they were ready to face it together. Their bond was unbreakable, and the experiences they had shared in the enchanted forest had strengthened their resolve.

"Let's make sure we're prepared for whatever comes our way," Alex said, echoing their shared sentiment. "Our adventure isn't over yet, and we need to be vigilant."

Christine added, "We've learned so much on this journey, not just about ourselves but about the world around us. We can handle anything that comes our way."

Celine chimed in, her voice filled with determination. "Asena may be gone for now, but we'll find her and set things right. We're the guardians, and we won't let any challenge stand in our way."

With unwavering unity, the guardians continued their path toward the city, ready to face the mysteries that awaited them and determined to ensure that peace and balance would return to their world.

As the guardians left the enchanted forest behind and headed back towards their homes, they couldn't help but appreciate the beauty of the world around them. The sun painted the sky with shades of orange and pink, casting a warm, golden light over the landscape. The rolling hills and serene meadows were a testament to the wonders of nature.

Alex, usually the tech-savvy guardian, found himself drawn to the beauty of the natural world. He gazed at the fields of wildflowers that stretched as far as the eye could see. The vibrant colours and the gentle sway of the blossoms in the breeze were a sight to behold. "You know, nature is pretty amazing," he mused. "I've spent so much time with gadgets and screens, but there's something magical about this."

Christine couldn't agree more. "It's like a painting come to life," she said. "I never really appreciated it until now."

Celine, always in tune with her surroundings, couldn't help but feel the energy of the world around her. "Nature has its own rhythm and beauty," she said with a smile. "It's a symphony of life, and we're part of it."

The guardians continued to enjoy their journey back, often pausing to take in the simple pleasures of the world. They laughed, they played, and they felt a deep sense of connection with each other and the world around them. It was a moment of respite, a reminder of the joy that life could bring.

They reached their homes, and while their adventure in the enchanted forest was over, they knew that they had changed. They had grown closer as friends, found strength within themselves, and discovered a newfound appreciation for the beauty of nature.

As the sun set on their adventure, they felt a sense of contentment. The world was full of wonders, and they were ready to embrace whatever the future held, knowing that they were the guardians of a world filled with magic and mystery.

The guardians made their way back to the city, where life was bustling with people going about their daily routines. As they approached their neighbourhood, the familiar sights and sounds of home filled their senses.

As they entered the neighbourhood, they couldn't help but feel a sense of nostalgia and anticipation. It had been quite some time since they had seen their parents, and the thought of reuniting with their families warmed their hearts.

When they reached their respective homes, their parents were waiting with open arms. Tears of joy welled up in their eyes as they rushed to embrace each other.

Hugs were shared, laughter filled the air, and the sense of belonging was palpable.

Inside their homes, the guardians recounted their incredible journey in the enchanted forest. Their parents listened with amazement, hanging on to every word. It was a tale of adventure, bravery, and the unbreakable bond of friendship.

The evening was filled with shared stories, hearty meals, and a sense of completeness. The guardians had returned, and they were surrounded by the love and warmth of their families.

As they settled back into the comforts of home, they couldn't help but reflect on their magical adventure. The enchanted forest had changed them, and now, with their families by their side, they were ready to face whatever challenges and wonders the future might bring.

The following morning, as the city stirred to life, the shop owner realized that some of their belongings had gone missing. It was a matter of concern, and they voiced their distress loudly. People gathered around, offering their sympathies and discussing the incident.

Amidst the commotion, Alex felt responsible, knowing that the guardians had taken some items from the shop during their quest. Feeling guilty and wanting to make amends, he approached the shop owner and handed them $15 as compensation for the trouble caused.

The shop owner, surprised by Alex's honesty and sincerity, accepted the money with gratitude. They understood that it was not an act of theft but rather an unforeseen circumstance brought about by the magical journey of the guardians. In the end, this gesture of goodwill from Alex helped mend any ill feelings and left a positive impression on the shop owner and the community.

With this final act of kindness, the guardians' adventure came to a close, and they returned to the routines and responsibilities of their everyday lives, carrying the lessons and experiences of the enchanted forest with them.

With their grand adventure behind them, the three friends returned to the ordinary world of school and studies. As they entered the classroom, their teacher announced that it was time for them to select the subjects they would pursue in their future education. This was a significant step toward their academic and career goals.

Alex, who had once been primarily interested in technology and IT, surprised everyone by choosing Nature and IT. His time in the enchanted forest had ignited a newfound appreciation for the wonders of the natural world, and he decided to merge his technological skills with his love for nature.

Celine, with her passion for literature and the environment, opted for Nature and Literature, finding a way to blend her love for storytelling with her dedication to preserving the environment.

Christine chose Nature and Commerce, emphasizing the importance of sustainable business practices and eco-friendly entrepreneurship in the modern world.

Their choices reflected the profound impact that their magical journey had on them, transforming their interests and aspirations. The three friends laughed together, marvelling at how much they had changed and grown. Their adventure had not only strengthened their bond but had also shaped their future paths in a way they could never have predicted.

With newfound determination and purpose, they embarked on their educational journey, eager to explore and contribute to the world around them. Their time in the enchanted forest had left an indelible mark on their hearts and minds, inspiring them to embrace the beauty of nature and the power of knowledge in their pursuit of a brighter future.

Asena, having vanished from the scene, now appeared in a secret and hidden place, cloaked in a mysterious hoodie. Her expression was determined and relentless. She knew that her journey was far from over, and she had more plans in mind.

With a wave of her staff, she cast a spell, and a dark, enigmatic light enveloped her. It was a harbinger of her return, a promise that her quest was far from finished. Asena had tasted defeat, but she remained unyielding, a formidable force that would continue to pursue her ambitions, no matter the cost. The dark aura she summoned symbolized her unyielding determination to achieve her goals, and the world would surely feel her presence once again.

KNOW THIS

I WILL RETURN!

END OF A CHAPTER

ACKNOWLEDGMENT

*I am deeply grateful to the following individuals whose unwavering support, encourage
and inspiration made this novel possible:*

Family and Friends:

To my family, for their patience and understanding throughout countless late
nights and weekends spent at my desk. Your love and belief in me sustained my
creative spirit. To my friends, who provided both encouragement and a listening
ear, thank you for always being there. And for providing countless information and
methods

Mentors and Writing Community:

I want to express my appreciation to the Wattpad community, whose guidance
and wisdom have been invaluable on this writing journey.

Beta readers and teachers:

A heartfelt thank you to my English and English literature teacher, whose keen eye
and valuable insights have polished this manuscript. your feedback was
instrumental in shaping this novel into its final form. And for the countless
suggestions that helped me countless times

*To every reader who picks up this book, thank you for embarking on this journey with r
Your enthusiasm and support mean the world to me.*

by Rashmitha Jayawardhana